NEARLY SAFE

(A Grace Ford FBI Suspense Thriller—Book 2)

Molly Black

Molly Black

Bestselling author Molly Black is author of the MAYA GRAY FBI suspense thriller series, comprising nine books (and counting); of the RYLIE WOLF FBI suspense thriller series, comprising six books; of the TAYLOR SAGE FBI suspense thriller series, comprising eight books; of the KATIE WINTER FBI suspense thriller series, comprising eleven books (and counting); of the RUBY HUNTER FBI suspense thriller series, comprising five books (and counting); of the CAITLIN DARE FBI suspense thriller series, comprising five books (and counting); of the REESE LINK mystery series, comprising five books (and counting); of the CLAIRE KING FBI suspense thriller series, comprising five books (and counting); and of the GRACE FORD FBI suspense thriller series, comprising five books (and counting).

An avid reader and lifelong fan of the mystery and thriller genres, Molly loves to hear from you, so please feel free to visit www.mollyblackauthor.com to learn more and stay in touch.

ISBN: 978-1-0943-7931-9

BOOKS BY MOLLY BLACK

GRACE FORD MYSTERY SERIES
NEARLY MINE (Book #1)
NEARLY SAFE (Book #2)
NEARLY FREE (Book #3)
NEARLY GONE (Book #4)
NEARLY HIS (Book #5)

CLAIRE KING MYSTERY SERIES
ONCE HE SEES (Book #1)
ONCE HE LONGS (Book #2)
ONCE HE TAKES (Book #3)
ONCE HE FEELS (Book #4)
ONCE HE KNOWS (Book #5)

MAYA GRAY MYSTERY SERIES
GIRL ONE: MURDER (Book #1)
GIRL TWO: TAKEN (Book #2)
GIRL THREE: TRAPPED (Book #3)
GIRL FOUR: LURED (Book #4)
GIRL FIVE: BOUND (Book #5)
GIRL SIX: FORSAKEN (Book #6)
GIRL SEVEN: CRAVED (Book #7)
GIRL EIGHT: HUNTED (Book #8)
GIRL NINE: GONE (Book #9)

RYLIE WOLF FBI SUSPENSE THRILLER
FOUND YOU (Book #1)
CAUGHT YOU (Book #2)
SEE YOU (Book #3)
WANT YOU (Book #4)
TAKE YOU (Book #5)
DARE YOU (Book #6)

TAYLOR SAGE FBI SUSPENSE THRILLER
DON'T LOOK (Book #1)
DON'T BREATHE (Book #2)

DON'T RUN (Book #3)
DON'T FLINCH (Book #4)
DON'T REMEMBER (Book #5)
DON'T TELL (Book #6)

KATIE WINTER FBI SUSPENSE THRILLER
SAVE ME (Book #1)
REACH ME (Book #2)
HIDE ME (Book #3)
BELIEVE ME (Book #4)
HELP ME (Book #5)
FORGET ME (Book #6)
HOLD ME (Book #7)
PROTECT ME (Book #8)
REMEMBER ME (Book #9)
CATCH ME (Book #10)
WATCH ME (Book #11)

RUBY HUNTER FBI SUSPENSE THRILLER
IF I RUN (Book #1)
IF I TELL (Book #2)
IF I LIVE (Book #3)
IF I FORGET (Book #4)
IF I RETURN (Book #5)

CAITLIN DARE FBI SUSPENSE THRILLER
COME GET ME (Book #1)
COME FIND ME (Book #2)
COME TAKE ME (Book #3)
COME CATCH ME (Book #4)
COME SAVE ME (Book #5)

REESE LINK MYSTERY
BEYOND REASON (Book #1)
BEYOND REACH (Book #2)
BEYOND REPAIR (Book #3)
BEYOND DOUBT (Book #4)
BEYOND NORMAL (Book #5)

PROLOGUE

Parker Menzies knew he shouldn't be here, down at the river. It could be a dangerous move.

Especially today.

He looked around furtively as he made his way down the slippery, muddy path, to a part of the river that was secluded, with reeds and bushes shielding it from sight. He felt a guilty twist of pleasure in his belly at what he was about to do.

His boss, Mr. Worth, would be spitting mad if he knew he was here now. It was close to the month's end, and that always meant more pressure, more customers needing their accounts up to date, more payroll changes. A pile of work was waiting for him in the office, including a few urgent jobs.

Parker might be only twenty-two years old, but he'd realized, early on in his job as a junior bookkeeper working for Worth Business Management, that Mr. Worth seemed to have eyes in the back of his head when it came to his staff's activities. He could get into big trouble now.

But after days of nonstop rain, a winter storm that had swept through Arkansas, it was finally a glorious day.

Cold, bright, clear, and he hadn't been able to resist detouring from the breakfast meeting with a client, to cast a few flies. Seeing as how his gear happened to be in his trunk, and his route led him straight past this out-of-the-way, and particularly good, fishing ground.

The river gleamed in the low morning sun, wide and silvery blue, and although the deeper parts would be moving fast, swollen by the rain, the shallows were calmer.

Parker took a deep breath, inhaling the crisp, fresh air. He closed his eyes and let the sun warm his face. The stress and pressure from work began to melt away, and he felt a sense of peace wash over him. He had always loved fishing, and it was his go-to activity when he needed to clear his head.

He cast his line and waited patiently. The only sounds were the soft gurgles of the river and the occasional birdsong. It was perfect. Just him, the river, and the fish.

Although, what was that rustling noise from beyond the trees?

Distracted from the rhythm of casting his line, Parker's head jerked up and he stared anxiously in that direction. The line fluttered down, his momentum broken, the fly dropping into the reeds.

It was his own guilty conscience, Parker decided. For a moment, he'd thought there was somebody there, watching from behind the trees. His imagination had conjured up Mr. Worth himself, crouching behind a solid trunk, eyeing him with that stonily patient gaze he had that signaled trouble would follow.

Parker shook his head, chiding himself for letting his imagination get the best of him, realizing how silly it was to be afraid of his boss stalking him in the middle of nowhere.

He reeled in his line and started to cast again, his focus returning to the task at hand. But then he heard the rustling, closer this time.

He glanced that way again.

It was probably nothing. Maybe just a small animal moving through this section of dense undergrowth. But he couldn't shake the feeling of unease he felt. He had a definite certainty he was being watched.

Now, he remembered with a shiver that there had been reports of trouble, a few months ago, near the river. Cars being broken into when they were parked, and one woman had reported being harassed by a stranger who'd followed her.

Okay, that had been toward the end of summer, and they had caught the drifter who was responsible, but what if there was someone else out here now?

What if somebody was watching now? What if some criminal was waiting in the undergrowth, checking him out, planning on breaking into his car, or even doing something worse? What would he do if his car was stolen from the river, with all those important and confidential client files inside that he was supposed to take straight back to the office?

Parker grimaced. Now that his imagination was racing ahead, he was finding it impossible to enjoy his fishing. The feeling of uneasy guilt was too strong.

And then, an idea came to him that seemed perfect in its clarity. He could simply walk over to the bushes and check if anyone was there. He'd always had the mindset that it was better to take the initiative, because most times if you did that, you found it was just your fears getting the better of you.

After all, what could go wrong?

Parker put down his rod, and waded back toward the riverbank, his eyes scanning the surrounding bushes for any sign of movement. The rustling was closer now, and he knew for certain that someone or something was there.

With each step, his apprehension grew, but he couldn't shake off the feeling that he needed to investigate, to root out whatever it was. His instincts had always been sharp, and he trusted them now more than ever.

Suddenly, a twig snapped behind him. Parker spun around, his hand instinctively reaching for his missing knife.

Nothing there. Just a tree branch, finally giving way with a crack. That was all.

He continued on, now out of the shallows and into the mud, which tugged and sucked at his waders as he plowed his way toward that outcrop of trees.

It couldn't be a bear, could it? Surely not: surely the bears around here weren't active during winter? Maybe it was just a deer.

It couldn't be a person, he told himself firmly. His imagination had been wrong. It must have been. What would a person be doing, lurking in the trees like that?

Parker reached the top of the bank, his heart pounding in his chest. He walked slowly, cautiously, trying to keep his footsteps as quiet as possible.

He was almost at the edge of the tree line now. He paused, putting his hand on the rough bark of a large tree to steady himself.

And then, with a crash that caused him to let out a cry of fear, the large deer that had been cautiously eyeing him erupted from the undergrowth.

Parker stumbled back, breathing hard, adrenaline still surging. He tripped over something solid, landing on his backside in the stinking mud, with an undertone of rot and decay, heart still pounding from that sudden fright.

Just a deer. That was all it had been. The spooky feeling had been for nothing.

He picked himself up, feeling ashamed, and that he'd been punished by life for his laziness in having skipped work. This was what he deserved. His mother always said karma would get her own revenge.

And now, he was going to get back to work, after having gotten rid of all the mud streaking his arms. He wasn't one to ignore a stern message from karma, or the guilty clamoring of his subconscious.

But as he scrambled up, he looked down to see exactly what it was that he'd fallen over.

It had seemed like a thick, solid branch or a tree root, but the smell of rot was even stronger.

And, as he backed away and stared down, Parker realized why.

A leg - a human leg - pale and bluish-white, was jutting out of the ground.

He'd fallen over a body.

Parker's stomach lurched as he scrambled back, trying to regain his footing on the slippery mud. It couldn't be real. It had to be some sort of sick joke or a Halloween prop that had been left there. It couldn't be a human leg jutting out of the ground.

"What the hell?" His voice sounded like a stranger's, high and shrill as he shouted the words.

It was real. There was the leg, and he could see the outline of arms, too. What had happened? Had this person drowned?

As he looked closer at what the waters had uncovered from this shallow grave, he felt his sense of horror intensify.

The arms were tied together, taut ropes trussing the wrists, digging into the pale and bloated flesh.

This was no accident; this was not drowning.

This was murder.

CHAPTER ONE

FBI agent Grace Ford stared across the kitchen table at her boyfriend, Tyler. She was about to speak the four words that she knew would start a fight.

She was ready. She took a deep breath. Having agonized over this for days, she had finally made up her mind, and it wasn't going to be the decision he expected. But it was the right decision. That, she was sure of.

"I'm taking the job," she said firmly.

Tyler's handsome face tautened in consternation. His hand clutched the edge of the polished wooden surface, looking as if he was about to jump to his feet. The table wobbled, sending coffee splashing.

Tyler had just poured his own coffee. His hair was still damp, brushed back from his post-gym shower. He'd gotten back home a minute ago from his morning workout.

"I thought you weren't going to! You said yesterday you were thinking of turning it down."

Grace put down her half-finished cup, and shook her head. Her long brown hair, tied back in a ponytail, swung back and forth. She narrowed her hazel green eyes as she focused her stare.

"I said that for the wrong reasons, Tyler, and that's what I realized this morning when I woke up."

She didn't add that it was why she mostly hadn't slept. She'd truly been fretting over this decision, with her answer due before the start of work today.

The job, which was causing so much conflict, was the offer of a permanent role with the new FBI task force specializing in fighting crime along the Mississippi River.

"The wrong reasons?" Tyler's voice rose, incredulously, as he spoke. "What are these wrong reasons?"

Grace sighed. "To prevent getting into a fight with you. And the fact that I was about to make a decision affecting my entire career future, based on the fact that it would stop an argument from starting, told me that I should rethink it. So I did."

"But - but -" Tyler looked appalled. He frowned, the expression making his chiseled face look surprisingly petulant. "But it's going to mean you spend time away from me!"

"We've had this conversation already," Grace said. "If our relationship can't survive the fact that I might be out of state one or two weeks during in the month, then it's not much of a relationship. I've always been an FBI agent, Tyler, from the get-go of our relationship. You knew that when we started dating. And I told you, at the start, that I was lucky to have been based in one place for so long, because agents do get transferred. Regularly. At any time, the director might make a decision to shuffle staff, and I might get deployed to LA, or to Florida, or to - to Alaska. And I couldn't refuse that transfer request. What would you do if that happened?"

She stared at him, feeling anger surge, because he was shaking his head stubbornly, being unreasonable.

"You're talking about a hypothetical situation," he retorted.

"So let's talk about the real one then. For now, I've been offered this job. Fighting crime along the river. And in the meantime, in my downtime, I'll still be based in Minnesota, which is a piece of luck for us."

"You said that you were going to put us first," he insisted.

"You said you were going to book yourself in for counseling sessions, to address your issues about making a permanent commitment," Grace retorted. "You haven't done that, have you? So we're still in a situation where marriage is not on the table because you're not ready to go there. And you haven't yet gotten help for your issues. Right?"

She stared around the apartment's living area, taking in the decor, the furniture they had bought together, the items she'd chosen herself, the pieces he'd come back with. The picture on the wall, a seascape, had been her choice. The rug on the floor in vivid blue, they'd chosen together. The curtains, bright white, had been inherited from Tyler's old apartment when they moved in together.

Suddenly, Grace realized, she was seeing this apartment not as a cohesive whole, but as a jigsaw puzzle that could be dismantled and put into its separate pieces again, at any moment. His and hers. Taking the links that had connected their lives together and pulling them apart.

It was a strange, disorienting feeling, and she didn't like it.

But deep down, she also wasn't going to deny it. This was ultimately where their relationship might be heading.

Tyler looked down. "I'm planning on going to counseling. I've just been busy. My work's been hectic, you know."

"And so has mine. These crimes along the Mississippi River are escalating, and I want to be a part of the team that stops them. But yet, you're asking me to stay here and turn down a career opportunity so that I spend seven nights a week at home?"

Tyler shook his head, his eyes focused on the table. "No, of course not. It's just hard for me to accept that you'll be away so much. I mean, isn't it good that I want us to be together?"

He wanted them to be together, but yet he'd shared with her that he had commitment issues, that experiences in his earlier life made it difficult for him to take the next step in their relationship.

He wanted togetherness but she was now wondering if that offer to go for counseling had been nothing more than lip service, never seriously meant. And that was worrying her. She wasn't going to allow herself to stay in a one-sided relationship. She'd never minded his nights out of town or out of state for his work. She'd always felt glad that he had the opportunity to travel.

He didn't feel the same way, and now she was wondering if it was more of a control issue. Or just an evasion. Perhaps, because of his own personal challenges with commitment, he wanted her to stay here because it meant he didn't have to address his problems in bigger ways.

It was an unsettling thought, but one she couldn't budge now that it had lodged in her mind.

This relationship was important to her, but she couldn't sacrifice her career for it. She needed to keep her own future with the FBI in mind, even if that meant being away from Tyler for extended periods of time. She had always been open and upfront about the nature of her job, and if he couldn't handle it, then maybe it was time to re-evaluate the relationship.

"Tyler, I love you. I really do. But I can't put my career on hold for anyone. Not even for you. And it's unfair for you to ask me to do that."

Tyler looked up at her, his eyes filled with hurt. "I'm not asking you to put your career on hold. Surely you can turn down the offer, and carry on as you are?"

Grace let out a deep sigh and shook her head. "No, Tyler. I can't turn down the offer. This is a huge opportunity for me, and I know they've asked me because I have the skills to make it work. This is fighting crime. It's a life and death issue. If I get this right and do my job, I can save lives. I can prevent people using the river as an easy way to commit serious interstate crimes without being caught, and that's something we're seeing a spike in right now."

He nodded reluctantly.

"I want to be a part of something bigger, something that makes a difference."

"Maybe you don't want to be a part of this relationship then," he said angrily, and Grace felt her own temper flare again. She'd literally explained the situation to him word for word, and he was refusing to see it, choosing only to look at his side.

"I never said that, Tyler. I just need you to understand that my career is important to me too. If you can't support me in that, then I don't know where that leaves us," Grace said firmly.

"You should have spoken to me before you said yes," Tyler insisted, and now Grace felt herself get mad. Really, really mad. That was unacceptable. What Tyler had just said - that she should have looked for his permission before making a career choice - was not fair in her book.

She took a deep breath, knowing the time for being reasonable had almost passed, and that she was probably going to regret what she said to him next.

But then, as she was about to blurt out the angry words, her phone rang.

She'd put it in her jacket pocket after calling her boss, Zach Casteel, earlier that morning. She'd made the call to accept the job while standing out in the freezing cold on the balcony, after taking a walk to get her head straight.

Now, Zach was calling again.

"I have to take this. It's work," she said.

She heard Tyler sigh, deliberately loud, as she turned away, walking through to the bedroom to take the call in private.

"Zach?" she asked.

"Grace," he replied. "Glad you agreed to joining the task force, because we've just had a new case land. It's down in Arkansas. Two bodies have been found in the last three days, half buried on the river bank, both murdered, and a similar MO. The second one was found half an hour ago, and I've just had the call from the local PD."

As she listened to the words, Grace felt her pulse quicken.

Arkansas?

That was the state where her mother had been murdered, when Grace was seventeen years old. Her mother had been killed on her annual trip to visit her cousins who lived there. Grace's world had shattered after that news. She'd never been to Arkansas. It had always felt tainted by that terrible, inexplicable crime. Now, she was being asked to investigate a new killer, in a state where trouble felt worryingly close to home.

"How soon can you get to the airport?" Zach asked, his voice questioning, as if he was wondering about her silence.

"I can be there in half an hour," Grace said firmly, putting the memories of her mother to the back of her mind. She picked up her carry-on bag, which she'd already packed in preparation for short-notice trips, after she'd called him earlier.

She wanted to ask Zach for more detail - in particular, who she'd be partnered with. Her mind veered immediately to the tall, rangy Dylan Reed, who'd been her partner on the first river case she'd handled. Would he be part of the task force? Had he also received the same offer she had?

There wasn't time to ask, because after thanking her, and telling her he'd send her more details, Zach hung up in a hurry.

Carrying the bag, she went through to the dining room, where Tyler was now texting on his phone, still looking mutinous.

"I've got a case. In Arkansas. I'll be in touch later," she said.

He didn't answer.

His silence spoke louder than words as Grace headed out into the freezing morning, forcing her thoughts to the case ahead, and not on the problems she was leaving behind.

CHAPTER TWO

"New place, new start," FBI agent Dylan Reed said aloud, looking around his bachelor pad, a third-story apartment in Baton Rouge, Louisiana. The fake cheer resounded in his voice discordantly.

He was trying to seek the positives in what felt like an overwhelmingly negative situation.

They said divorce was hard, but he was feeling brutalized by it, punished by the flood of emotion and by the harrowing task of packing up his life as he'd known it.

It hadn't felt like divorce. More like getting crushed by an avalanche, in fact.

The only good thing about it, he guessed, was that it had made it an easier decision to take on the new role with the specialized river-based FBI task force. That had been the only good thing to come out of this fortnight of hell.

He'd accepted unquestioningly when the director had called, and had given his response so fast that the director had asked, surprised, "Don't you need some time to think about it?"

"No," he'd said. "I've made up my mind already. Handling the first case was a challenge I enjoyed, and I felt it spoke to my strengths. I'll be very proud to take on the role."

As he accepted, he briefly wondered if agent Grace Ford, whom he'd worked with on the first case, would also be a part of the permanent task force.

He hoped she would, though he hadn't had much time to think about it.

He'd literally been speaking on the phone to accept this new role, while cramming underwear and socks into a gym bag ready for the big move out of his old home, where the broken shreds of his ruined marriage lay. That was the week he'd had in a nutshell.

Unpacking could happen at a slower pace, he hoped.

He'd been lucky, given the new role, that the bachelor pad he'd chosen was close to the airport. That would make travel easier.

More importantly, the apartment also had a view of the Mississippi River itself, which had sold Dylan on it, despite the rent being higher than he'd expected. There was something soothing and timeless about sitting on the balcony and watching the water flowing past a few hundred yards from him, watching the boats, the big cruisers, the smaller fishing boats.

Dylan had always felt a connection to water. It was a part of his childhood, growing up near the banks of a river in rural Louisiana. Fishing and boating had been a regular part of his life, and he was grateful for the view now as he started this new chapter.

It hadn't been a chapter he'd wanted to embark on.

He was in his early thirties, and five years ago, as a relative newlywed, he'd thought things would be very different.

Never had he imagined he'd be unpacking his things now, the number of boxes surprisingly meager, in this tiny, one bedroom space - which did, at least, have a great view going for it.

Never had he thought that a marriage that had started out with so much happiness and excitement could have first turned sour and then plummeted downhill when his wife, Valerie, had told him just two weeks ago that she'd been cheating on him and that she didn't want to fix their marriage. She wanted a divorce.

He still felt a complex mix of emotion whenever he thought about it, which of course, was almost all the damned time. Anger, shame, self-blame, despair.

Years of togetherness, of shared memories, were being put behind him now. The good times, the less good times. The hopes and dreams that had slowly settled into mundanity, and a sense of dissatisfaction punctuated by bitter fights and occasional resolutions that he must try harder. And then they had finally curdled into the realization that there would be nothing.

Dylan's phone rang as he was snipping open the tape on the third box, the one that contained his books.

It was his father, calling from his small-town home in rural Louisiana, and seeing his number on the screen brought Dylan a shred of comfort, but also a whole heap of other bad memories along with it.

His dad, in his late fifties, was tall and rangy, and surprisingly young looking - a family trait, Dylan knew. Only the lines around his dad's eyes, and the hardness of his face, gave away the tragedy that had occurred nearly fifteen years ago when Dylan's sister had gone missing on the river, and never been found.

His parents had divorced a few years later; his dad had never remarried and had lived alone since that time. Now, in a somber and downhearted frame of mind, Dylan wondered if that, too, was a family trait.

"Hey, son," his dad greeted him. "How's it going? You settled in yet?"

Dylan's grip tightened on his phone as he spoke to his father. "Getting there. Just unpacking now."

"I saw the photos you sent me. Place looks comfortable. I like the view."

"Yeah, the view is what sold me," Dylan agreed.

There was a moment of silence before his dad spoke again. "I know it's not easy, Dylan. But are you sure you're doing the right thing? You can't try again?"

Dylan felt a surge of frustration. He knew that his dad was remembering the loss of Lizzie, who'd disappeared while boating on the river with a group of friends. It had been a sad irony that their boat had capsized in an unseasonal summer flood, just a few miles from the Reeds' home. Although three of her friends had swum to safety, and a fourth had been found clinging to a tree during the search and rescue operation that followed, Lizzie had never been found.

So, his dad was speaking from the standpoint of someone who'd suffered permanent loss of a daughter and then the additional trauma of a divorce a few years later, which Dylan knew was as a direct result of that pain. He'd been left with unanswered questions and no closure. Of course he was going to plead for a second chance for his son.

But it was too soon, too raw, for Dylan to be able to respond calmly.

"Dad," Dylan said, feeling the anger bubbling up inside him. "You can't turn the clock back. Valerie cheated on me. She broke my trust. And then she demanded a divorce. How can I fix that?"

His dad sighed, and Dylan could hear the pain and sadness in the sound. "I just hate to see you go through this, son. It's not easy."

Dylan took a deep breath and tried to calm himself down. He knew that his dad meant well, even though his words were like salt in an open wound. "I know, Dad. I appreciate your concern. But I need to move on. And I can't try again. She made it very clear she won't."

There was a pause before his dad spoke again. "I understand, son. I just wish I could do more to help you."

Dylan felt a pang of guilt. He knew his dad had been through so much already, and he didn't want to burden him even more. "You're doing enough, Dad. Talking to you makes me feel better." That was not entirely truthful at this moment, but it was still the right thing to say. He just hoped his dad didn't trot out advice about getting back into the dating game. That would be too soon, and he'd have to shoot down the idea.

But then, Dylan heard the beep signaling a waiting call. "I have to go," he said, with some relief. "I'll call you back later. Work's on the line."

Quickly, he hung up and took the other incoming call.

It was from the FBI Minnesota office, and it was his new boss, Zach Casteel, calling.

"Reed," Zach said. "How soon can you get to the airport? We've got a suspected serial, the state governor's already cranking up the pressure, and we need to move fast."

"Give me an hour," he said. "Where am I heading?"

The answer surprised him.

"Memphis, Tennessee," Zach told him. "I've chartered you a helicopter there, and organized a rental car. I need you to pick up Grace Ford at the airport. She'll be partnering with you on this case. She's catching a plane now, and will land at ten a.m."

"I'll wait for her," Zach said, feeling pleased that he'd have the tough, sassy, and talented Grace along with him on this case.

He hung up, and grabbed his travel bag.

Unpacking would have to wait. There was a case to solve – and a killer to catch.

CHAPTER THREE

As the airplane touched down, Grace felt reassured that she was fully focused on this case. It didn't matter that she was now in the same state where her mother had been murdered. That tragedy had happened long ago, and although there had been no answers, she'd been able to bottle up the trauma deep inside herself.

Plus, the physical distance she now had from Minnesota was helping her gain some emotional distance from the problems with Tyler that she'd left behind.

She knew, from the message Zach had sent just before she'd boarded, that there was already serious pressure to solve this case. The state governor was leaning hard on the FBI. He wanted answers, and an arrest, and he wanted them fast.

With the Mississippi providing a border between the states of Arkansas and Tennessee, Grace had been booked on a flight direct to Memphis as the closest airport to the crime scene.

Now, she turned on her phone to find another message from Zach.

"Special Agent Reed will be meeting you."

Grace was surprised to find herself suppressing a grin. This was good news. Serious and pressured as this case might be, the tall, likable Dylan Reed had worked well with her on the last case - after what she had to admit had been a slightly false start. She gave a wry smile as she remembered his inadequate clothing, and the way he'd shivered his way through the freezing northern winter day as they'd battled to catch a serial killer.

She'd doubted Dylan's abilities at first. But as they worked together, she had begun to appreciate his intelligence and quick thinking, his bravery, and also his intuition. Even if some of his ideas had seemed to come out of left field, she was surprised by how relevant they had ended up being.

As a practical person who valued the qualities of logic and deductive thinking, it was a surprise to find that she had worked well with a dreamer, someone who was more right-brained than herself. But she had to admit, his qualities had complemented hers on the last case. And for this one they were going to need all the synergy they could get.

She felt a flicker of doubt. They hadn't known each other very long, and were two very different people. This case would be the real test of how good a partnership they really had.

Now, she was down here in the south, where the warmer air without the bitter edge of northerly cold was only the first of the many differences; she knew she was at a disadvantage. This was Dylan's home ground, not hers. That meant she would need to work even harder to prove herself.

With only a carry-on, she disembarked from the airplane and strode straight through to arrivals.

There he was. Unmistakable. His height alone made him easy to spot in a crowd and that was before you added in the warm blue eyes and the smile, which she returned as she headed toward him. He was a cute guy, she guessed, though she wasn't the least attracted to him in a romantic way. Just as well, seeing she had enough problems on that side for now.

"Hey there, Dylan Reed," she called out as she approached. "Nice to see a familiar face."

"Likewise," he said. Then, more hesitantly, as if testing out the waters between them, he said, "I'm pleased you took up the offer to join the task force."

She nodded, smiling. She was pleased that he had, too.

They walked through the airport. The silence between them felt slightly uncomfortable. They didn't know each other well enough yet for a sense of camaraderie to exist between them, Grace realized. She should probably make some conversation, get the dialogue flowing.

"Joining the task force wasn't an easy decision. I battled with it for a while," she admitted, realizing immediately that her attempt at chit-chat had resulted in giving out too much information. It hadn't hit the note of easy banter she'd intended.

"Why's that?" he asked as they headed to the exit. Grace hesitated, not wanting to say too much, and aware that saying anything might open those floodgates too wide.

"Mainly personal reasons. I had to put my own work priorities ahead of – ahead of other people's priorities," she hedged.

"Sounds like you had some conflict to work through?" he sympathized.

Just because he'd had a sympathetic response, though, didn't mean she was going to spill out all the details of her love life. That would be oversharing. She didn't feel comfortable with doing that, being a reserved person, who didn't naturally open up to others easily.

"I worked through it. Partially, at least. And I did what was right for my career," she said.

Dylan nodded understandingly, and she could tell he was curious, knowing that there was more to the story, but respecting her privacy.

"Sometimes life throws us curveballs, and we have to make difficult choices."

"And for you? Was the decision easy?" she asked.

He headed over to the silver Honda rental, with the FBI shield displayed in the window, parked in the yellow line area outside the exit. "It was easy for me. A no brainer, in fact. It was about the only thing that's gone right since - since we solved the last case."

Sitting in the passenger seat, Grace glanced at him, concerned by the bitterness in his tone. She was also curious now about what had transpired in his personal life. But since he'd given her space and hadn't pressured her with questions, she had to do the same.

But she was going to find out more. She promised herself that.

For now though, with the chit chat over - such as it was - there were more important topics to discuss.

"Are we going straight to the latest crime scene?" she asked, remembering that Zach's brief information had stated that the second body was discovered earlier this morning.

He nodded. "Police are still there. They're wrapping up, I believe, but I'd like to get a feel for the location. I got us a radio from the police station on the way, so we can keep in communication quickly when we need to."

The familiar crackle of the radio sounded loud in the rental car, but Grace felt glad they had that line of communication available. Especially seeing as they would need to work closely with the local police.

She opened her phone to find that an email had come through from Zach while she'd been in the air. Now was as good a time as any to summarize the case for both their benefit.

"Okay. Shall I read through the report?" she said.

Dylan nodded. "Sure. I've already read it, but you go ahead."

She glanced at him frowning. Was he saying she shouldn't read it out loud?

Well, she was going to. She wanted to get this logically summarized, and to piece together the sequence in her mind.

Feeling slightly awkward at his lack of enthusiasm - although perhaps it was just the doubts and nerves of starting this important case that were making her feel that way - she started reading.

"Two days ago, a body was found in the shallows, in Arkansas, half buried in the mud. Body was of a man, age twenty-six. Bound and gagged, cause of death was drowning."

"Victim was IDed, I believe," Dylan added.

Grace nodded, scrolling through the email. "Yes, his name is Thomas Lane. He was from Little Rock, and had been reported missing by his family three days ago."

"And now this one, discovered early this morning by a fisherman," Dylan said. "It seems like the same MO, but details are sketchy."

He was driving out of town, and Grace took a look around, watching as he crossed over the bridge, and into Arkansas, taking the main road south. Quickly, the urban scenery melted into deepest countryside. The road ran roughly parallel to the river for a few miles, before veering away from it. They passed an enormous lake next to the river, the sunlight glinting off the water.

The area was crammed full of natural beauty, but it was all the more disturbing to her that somewhere within this idyllic scenery, a killer was at work. An angry killer. Bodies trussed, bound, gagged. Why had he done that? Was it something to do with making them feel helpless?

She shook her head, thoughts of her mother's death briefly crowding in again.

Firmly, she banished them, and told herself that they were now going to stay away. She needed to focus on this case. She couldn't allow herself to become haunted because she was in the state where a terrible, inexplicable crime had occurred more than a decade ago.

As Dylan glanced at his GPS, driving off the narrow strip of asphalt and onto a dirt track, she knew they were close to the scene.

The flashing lights of the police cars grew brighter as they approached, and she saw the familiar yellow tape cordoning off the area, which looked bushy and overgrown. They parked the car and got out, showing their badges to the police officers on duty.

A rusty signboard indicated: Swimming, Fishing. But it seemed from the remoteness of the area and the state of the track that people didn't do that very often here.

Grace could already hear the rushing of water from the river beyond. She breathed in the air - cold, and with a leafy freshness. She picked up an undertone of rich-smelling, muddy loam.

"The air smells so pure here," she commented, thinking of the air she usually breathed, which was tainted with gas fumes and always seemed filled with smoke.

"Better than the water," Dylan commented with a grimace. "That's not as clear and pure as it should be."

"How do you know?" Grace asked.

"I follow the news in the wider area, and I've always had an interest in the river since I grew up in a riverside town. So I've read and heard that there are ongoing issues with the water quality. Have been for years, and they're complex. Not easy to solve."

Turning onto the muddy, narrow path that led down to the river, Dylan led the way, and Grace followed closely behind him. As they stepped over the yellow tape strung between two trees, Grace felt a chill run down her spine.

The body was gone, she saw, although white-clad forensic officers were combing the scene. But there was a sense of foreboding about this site, shielded from the world, thickly surrounded by trees and bushes, and with the deep, glutinous mud flanked by rushing water.

Breathing it in, after what Dylan had said, Grace did think she picked up a sour smell coming off the water as she put her foot covers on before approaching the scene.

It was a place that looked somewhat ideal for a killer's choice. And at that moment, a shout came from the place near the river bank.

"Got something! Here!"

She and Dylan glanced at each other, eyes wide. Then, they hustled down to the riverbed.

CHAPTER FOUR

"Agents Ford and Reed," Grace introduced the two of them breathlessly as she and Dylan scrambled down the muddy bank. The police officer in charge - at any rate, she guessed so - was also bustling over to the scene where the forensic officer had made a find.

What would he have found? She hoped it was something that would give them a lead. In this environment, with vast spaces and swiftly moving water, they would need to get lucky to find something. Maybe they had gotten lucky?

The police officer paused when he saw them, and swung around.

"I'm Detective Stoll. It's good to have you on board with this, agents. We've been investigating the backgrounds, and we've put an appeal out to the public for any information, but so far, there are no obvious suspects for these crimes."

Grace hesitated, staring at the detective, with his graying hair and bushy mustache and a sense of deliberateness about his actions. There was something about Stoll's tone and demeanor that rung bells in her mind. His greeting had been polite enough, and he didn't seem to resent them being here, which had been her worst fear. But all the same, there was something that struck a wrong note with her.

No time to think about that now, though.

The forensic officer, working in the mud, was holding something up. It was a muddied rag, grimy and dripping with water.

"It's a gag, I think," he said. "I found it buried here, close to where the victim's head was resting. It might have come off when he was buried."

Dylan stepped forward to examine the rag, crouching down beside the forensic officer as he took a closer look. Grace could see the intensity in his expression, the way his eyes narrowed as he tried to make sense of what he was seeing.

"What's it made of? Any leads there?" he asked.

"I believe the original one, found on the first victim, was a piece of twisted cotton, but it had cotton wool stuffed inside it," the forensic officer said, his eyes sharp and blue over his mask. "This is the same, I think. It's heavy."

He lifted the dripping item and placed it carefully in an evidence bag.

"Cotton wool?" Grace asked. That intrigued her. Why would a killer do such a thing? Had it been to make sure that any shouts were muffled? If so, there were better ways of doing that than using cotton wool.

"Strange," Dylan muttered. She wondered if he would have some ideas about why this was used. She thought she should probably come up with ideas herself. But she couldn't figure it out.

Unless...

"Let's get it tested," she said. "Might be that we can get some trace evidence from it, if it's been buried in the mud."

"Yeah," Dylan said, rubbing his chin as he expanded on her theory. "I wonder if he was using something on that cotton wool? Could be something to make them choke, to make them die faster. Or something nasty tasting or smelling, to torture them?"

Grace's eyebrows rose. Those were very interesting, if chilling, ideas. Not only did they give her a potential window into this crime scene, but also into Dylan Reed's mind. Definitely unlike any other partner she'd had before.

It seemed that this was about all that the crime scene was going to yield, and Grace knew they were lucky to have found it, thanks to the forensic officer's diligent searching. Perhaps it would mean a breakthrough. Perhaps it would mean nothing. She didn't know.

"If the body's already at the coroner, I guess that should be our next stop?" she asked.

“I was thinking we should investigate the first victim’s contacts.”

“We can do that next,” she said, feeling worried that there was already some discord between them. But it didn’t turn into a fight. Dylan simply shrugged.

"Okay. Let's go see what the pathologist has to say. I know the area fairly well; I worked here a few years ago on a double murder case. If the offices are where they used to be, I won’t even need a map to get there," he said.

*

As they drove to the pathologist's office, Grace realized, again, how much like a fish out of water she felt in this part of the world. It was making her realize how much of a comfort zone she'd created for herself up in Haverton, Minnesota. She'd gone to the office every day. She knew where everything was: the closest police departments, the pathology offices in the area, the nearest prisons, the known bad spots, and problem areas.

It didn't do for any FBI agent to get too comfortable with their surroundings. As Dylan drove the ten-mile journey from memory to the pathology lab closest to this part of river where the two victims had been taken, she gazed out of the window, taking in the scenery, the character of the area, the way that the deep rural landscape gave way to a town whose name she'd never heard of before. And buried in a network of streets was the pathologist's office, located between a small day clinic and a steelworks factory.

"Sander is a small town, even by local standards, but the pathology office was located here because it was close to the main road. That was later rerouted, but nothing else changed," Dylan said, stopping outside the gate.

They walked inside, and immediately the temperature dropped, feeling much more like a Minnesota winter all over again. And suddenly, Grace didn't feel so disoriented anymore.

The town might be different, but pathology offices all had the familiar, if rather uncomfortable, sameness about them. She breathed in the sharp smell of disinfectant, trying not to think about the underlying odors that her sensitive nose could discern, and feeling glad when the receptionist handed them masks.

The pathologist they were there to see was a woman named Dr. Rodriguez, and on hearing her name, Dylan gave a nod of recognition. As they headed to the door that the receptionist pointed out, Dylan knocked briefly before opening it. Walking inside, Grace saw that the pathologist was petite and looked to be in her mid-forties, with short hair, and a lab coat that had seen better days. Her eyes above the mask were dark and intelligent.

"How's things going, Doc?" Dylan asked. "This is Grace Ford, from up north, working with me on the river crimes."

Dr. Rodriguez nodded in greeting, her expression professional yet friendly. "Good to see you again, Reed, and good to meet you, Agent Ford. Please, come in." She gestured for them to enter the small examination room.

"Is the postmortem complete?" Dylan asked her.

"I just finished it," she said. "I prioritized it, as it's a suspected serial. And the examination definitely confirmed that."

"So, what can you tell us about the victims?" Dylan asked, getting straight to the point.

"We haven't yet identified the second victim, but I know Detective Stoll was heading to the police station to take a look at the missing persons reports and see if anything matches up. His prints aren't in the system," she said.

"And the cause of death?"

"There was blunt force trauma to the back of their heads in both cases, so they were attacked from behind; but to me, the trauma is not sufficient to have killed them," the doctor said. "They died by drowning. Lungs filled with water, all the classic signs. Obviously gagged, and with their hands tied, it would have happened fast, especially if they had been knocked out first."

Grace winced at the thought of such a brutal attack. "What about those gags?" she asked.

Dr. Rodriguez looked at her, her expression serious. "They were made of twisted cotton, and stuffed with cotton wool. There was nothing unusual about the material itself, but I have sent them in for analysis as I believe you requested. The first one was saturated with water, but the second had been buried in the mud. It might hold traces of something. Perhaps the testing will tell us more."

"And the burial? Do you think they were purposely buried, or that they just ended up in the mud?" Grace asked. It was a question that had been weighing on her mind.

"I would say, from the level of saturation, that the first victim spent more time in the water. So I would say that man was not purposely buried. The other one might have been dumped closer to shore, and drifted there within a shorter time. He definitely spent less time in the water," she said.

"Is there anything else that might give us a lead on the killer?" Grace asked, but the doctor shook her head apologetically.

"I'll let you know about the test results as soon as I have them," she said.

With that finalized, but still frustratingly inconclusive, it was time to find out more about the first victim, Thomas Lane.

Tracking his movements, his recent interactions, and any trouble in his life, might get them closer to this killer.

CHAPTER FIVE

"Let's start by looking into Thomas Lane's background," Dylan said to Grace. "He's in his mid-twenties. And I see on the police records that he's listed here as being recently divorced. Maybe there was some trouble there?"

He felt for the guy. Being recently divorced himself - as of now - he was appreciating the amount of stress it brought. Perhaps Thomas had ended up in conflict with somebody. Maybe not even his wife, but a relative, a coworker - perhaps he'd exploded at the wrong person and let out his anger, with dire consequences.

That wrong person surely must have links to both victims. With two bodies discovered in the same local area, they had to assume there were common factors, and look at every facet they could.

"This divorce," Grace said, and he was pleased that she was clearly on the same page. "Maybe it caused conflict. I see he lived alone, but I'm looking in the databases and I see there's a Lane family, his relatives, just a couple of doors down."

Dylan tapped keys, going further into the local police records.

"Yes. It looks like that property he moved into is owned by his parents. They own all three houses in that strip on Ashford Road. The middle one is occupied by tenants."

"Interesting," Grace commented. "Maybe we should talk to his parents first. See if they were close to him, which I'm hoping they were if they lived so nearby. They might know more about the divorce, and what else was going on in his life."

Dylan nodded in agreement. "It's worth a shot. Let's start with the parents."

The drive was short, and they soon arrived at the Lane family's main property. The house was a modest, single-story building with a small garden out front. Dylan noticed that the lawn was immaculately mowed and the flower beds were well-tended. It gave the impression of a neat and tidy family, with everything in its proper place.

He glanced to the left, seeing that this home was the best maintained of the three houses in the line. The others, not so much.

Their yards were average to messy. The tenant, and also Thomas, didn't seem to keep the same high standards.

As they headed to the front door, Grace drew in a deep breath and paused for a moment. He glanced at her inquiringly.

"The family," she explained. "This death was so recent. I guess I always take a moment and prepare myself beforehand, for what's to come."

Dylan felt surprised by this. "I do the same, only afterward," he admitted. "When I get out of the house, after speaking to close relatives of a victim, I always stand for a minute, and let myself come to terms with it."

He appreciated that Grace was also that person who felt real empathy for the people she dealt with. Being so focused and evidence driven, that side of her hadn't yet been apparent.

He rang the bell and they waited.

After a few moments, footsteps approached, and the door was opened by a man with graying hair, wearing a blue plaid shirt. Dylan immediately noted the pallor of his face, and the deep rings under his eyes.

"Good morning," Dylan said, making sure the sympathy he felt was audible in his voice as he showed his badge. "I'm so sorry to intrude at this time. We're from the special task force investigating this crime, and we wondered if we could get some background on Thomas?"

The man looked at them both for a long moment before nodding and stepping back from the door to allow them entry.

"Please, come in," he said, gesturing to the living room. "I'm his father. My wife and I have been waiting for answers. The police did talk to us yesterday, but of course, we'll help in any way we can."

The police did? That surprised Dylan because there had been no mention of it in the case file. He guessed that the reporting hadn't kept pace with the developments on the case.

Dylan and Grace followed the father inside, taking a seat on the couch, which was spotless, as Mr. Lane took the armchair opposite them.

"Please tell me about Thomas," Dylan said, with a glance at Grace to make sure they were on the same page as this interview started out. Grace glanced back, and then returned her gaze to Mr. Lane, with all her focus on him.

"He was a good son," Mr. Lane began, his voice tinged with emotion. "But he was going through a tough time. His divorce hit him hard. He was always such a family-oriented man, and when his marriage ended, he blamed himself."

"I can imagine that would be difficult," Grace said sympathetically.

"Did he have any trouble in his life, any conflict with anyone?" Dylan asked, getting straight to the point.

Mr. Lane shook his head. "No, not that I know of. Thomas wasn't someone who fought. He wasn't an aggressive person in any way. If he had a problem with anyone, he'd talk it over. We had dinner with him, once a week or so, and there were no problems that I knew of."

"What about his ex-wife?" Grace asked, her voice gentle.

Mr. Lane sighed. "They agreed, after a couple of difficult years, that they were too different, that they wanted different things out of life. Thomas was devastated by it at the time, but I guess the divorce was as amicable as something like that could be, with two young people involved. They both realized that they were better off apart. His ex-wife kept the house, which he agreed to."

"Were either of them seeing anyone else?"

"Not that I know of." Mr. Lane shook his head.

"Did Thomas have any financial issues that you know of?" Dylan asked, wondering if the divorce had put pressure on him from that side.

Mr. Lane frowned, deep in thought. "Not that I'm aware of. He seemed to be getting on with his life. He had a good job, and he was happy to rent from us until he found somewhere else to live permanently. He was ready to move on again."

"And his job?" Dylan asked.

"He was a factory foreman. He worked for Lewes Inc."

Dylan nodded in understanding, while seeing a blank expression on Grace's face. Remembering she wasn't from the area, he quickly filled her in.

"Lewes Inc. is a large manufacturer of industrial chemicals. Their headquarters are near here," he filled her in.

"Tell me about his job?" Grace asked.

"Well, he was happy with it, but I know he was hoping for a promotion. He didn't want to be in the manufacturing side, he wanted to be moved to logistics." Mr. Lane frowned, as if trying to recall the details. "I think he had a serious problem with someone at work a while ago. I remember he complained that someone was putting the pressure on him and bullying him, and that he was going to sort it out. I think he mentioned, more recently, that it had been sorted." He stared at them, hollow-eyed. "But that couldn't be a reason for this happening. I'm sure. Could it?"

Dylan shook his head, not able to commit to an answer one way or the other, but he personally felt that Mr. Lane had told them something worth investigating. "We can't rule anything out at this point, Mr. Lane. But it's important for us to know as much as we can. Do you know his name, the man he had a problem with?"

"No, I don't think Thomas ever told me."

He glanced again at Grace, to see if she wanted to ask anything more. She looked up from her notebook, where she'd been jotting down the details, and raised her eyebrows, glancing at the door. Dylan agreed. It was time to leave.

As they got up to leave, Mr. Lane stood up too, his face looking even more haggard, and his eyes pleading. "Please find out who did this to my son. He didn't deserve to die like this."

"We will do everything we can," Dylan promised before following Grace out of the house.

He felt as if he needed a moment now. Taking in that grieving father's emotion had been gutting.

But there was no time to waste. A serious problem at work was worth following up on, and all the more so since Thomas hadn't mentioned names. Why not? Had he been afraid to? And how had it been 'sorted?' Grace clearly thought so too.

"We need to get to Lewes Inc," she said. "This is the first real sign we've had of anything being wrong. And I want to find out more."

CHAPTER SIX

Lewes Inc. was a much bigger setup than Grace had expected. The concrete-walled compound of offices and factory buildings, set a couple of miles out of town, must have covered at least twenty acres, and perhaps more. At any rate, the high perimeter wall ran alongside the road for a good quarter mile before they arrived at the gate.

Her first thought, as she and Dylan showed their badges to the guard on duty, was that there was a lot of money in this company. Perhaps a bully had gone to extreme lengths to protect his well-paying job after Thomas had complained?

She hoped they would soon find out. Or maybe not so soon. The guard, a beefy looking man in his thirties, with a shaved head and a black uniform, didn't seem willing to let them past this gate.

"I'm sorry, but without an appointment, I can't let you in," he said, his voice firm. "Health and safety regulations." He looked pleased, Grace thought.

"We're with the FBI, investigating a recent homicide of one of your workers, Thomas Lane. We need to speak with his boss, and a few other people at this company. Do you know who his boss would be?" Grace asked.

The guard shrugged. "It's a big company. Hundreds of employees."

"He works on the factory floor, apparently."

"Might be that Mr. Meyerson is in charge of him, then."

"We need to speak to Mr. Meyerson, then," Grace said, noticing that Dylan was getting on the phone.

"I can't just let you in without permission," the guard insisted. His voice and his expression were surprisingly blank, as if he wasn't even wasting any energy on raising his eyebrows or changing his tone. Clearly the FBI wasn't even getting that from him.

"If we come back with a warrant, we're going to make life much more problematic for you," Grace explained, trying not to sound annoyed at his obstructive attitude. She thought he was the kind of man who'd probably feed off that emotion.

"Not my problem, ma'am," he simply said as she seethed inwardly.

It looked as if they really were going to have to come back with a warrant, but then Dylan turned back to them.

"I'm speaking to Mrs. Evans now. Bertha Evans. She's one of Mr. Meyerson's secretaries. She says it's no problem, they are all very concerned about Thomas's death and want to sort this out, and we can go straight in. Meyerson's office is the second building on the right, I believe? She said it's fine if you escort us to the building."

The guard hesitated. "Okay," he relented, and opened the boom. "You can park in that lot on the side. Then I'll walk you into the main building."

Feeling relieved, Grace watched as Dylan put his phone away, climbed back into the car, and they accelerated through the gate.

"That was good work," she said.

Dylan raised an eyebrow. "I didn't actually speak to her. Just found out her name, and where the office was. Didn't want to risk anyone else being as obstructive. It's better that we just pitch up at the door, right?"

Grace nodded, impressed and rather amused by Dylan's quick thinking and his creative skills. It might get them into trouble later, but for now, at least they were inside.

"The guard didn't mention if the police had been here," she said, feeling troubled as she remembered the gray-haired detective in charge. "It doesn't sound as if they have been?"

Dylan shook his head. "They surely must have investigated Thomas's workplace, if his body was found two days ago?"

"I'm not sure of anything right now," Grace muttered.

Dylan raised an eyebrow. "I guess we'll find out," he said.

Dylan parked the car in the designated lot, and they followed the guard into the main building. He pointed them in the direction of the reception desk, before going back to his post.

The interior was just as impressive as the exterior, with sleek modern decor in blue and gray, and a wide reception console that spanned the entire back wall, where three women were busily at work. The big windows on the right-hand side looked onto a square of groomed grass, beyond which a giant warehouse hulked. On the left, the wall was covered in photos of the chemical manufacturer's premises in earlier days.

Grace thought, from the photos, it was a few decades old and had recently expanded. It was clear that Lewes Inc. was a company with a lot of money to burn.

She walked over to the least busy looking, and the blondest, of the three receptionists, who greeted them with a smile somewhere between plastic and professional.

"How can I help?" she asked.

"We're here to see Mr. Meyerson. We're from the FBI, investigating the recent homicide of Thomas Lane, one of the company's workers," Grace said, flashing her badge. The receptionist's smile faltered for a moment before she composed herself and picked up the phone.

"Of course, let me see if he's available." She picked up the phone and dialed a number. After a brief exchange, she hung up and turned back to Grace and Dylan. "He will make time to see you now," she said. She motioned towards the elevators. "Mr. Meyerson's office is on the third floor, the last door on the right."

Grace and Dylan thanked the receptionist and headed towards the elevators. She felt glad that the stringent security at the gate was somewhat more relaxed now that they were inside the building itself, but this didn't mean things would be easy.

They rode up in the elevator and arrived at the third floor - sleek, immaculate, bluish-gray. This floor had impersonal looking, abstract artwork, with angular designs and silvery blue shades, in frames along the walls.

Grace tapped on the last door, and they waited.

In a moment, a woman's voice said, "Come in?"

Grace opened the door to reveal a spacious office, with a huge window overlooking the factory building. Two desks were positioned on either side, and at each, a secretary was working. One was dark-haired, with gold spectacles and a stern expression, with a nameplate on the desk that read 'Jones.' The other had permed, steel-gray hair and looked even less welcoming, and according to the 'Evans' nameplate on her desk, this was the woman whose name Dylan had found out.

Grace guessed that the door on the far wall led into Mr. Meyerson's personal office, but it was open and she wasn't sure if he was in there.

"You're with the FBI?" Bertha Evans asked in surprise as Grace showed her badge.

"Investigating Thomas Lane's murder, Ms. Evans," she said.

There was a subtle shift in the attitude within the room, and to her surprise, both women seemed suddenly less stern.

"I'm so glad that it's being looked into," Bertha said.

"Have the police not been here?" Grace asked.

She shook her head. "Not to my knowledge," she said.

Her dark-haired colleague nodded. "Not to mine either," she agreed.

Grace and Dylan exchanged a look, both of them sensing that something wasn't adding up. The fact that the police hadn't yet visited the workplace of a recent murder victim was very irregular. It raised red flags and made Grace wonder if there was something more going on behind the scenes.

"Where is Mr. Meyerson today?" Grace asked.

"He's over in the mixing plant," the secretary replied. "We're a couple of employees short there today."

At least she was getting information from them, Grace thought, knowing that Mr. Meyerson's arrival might complicate the situation, and that she should try to find out as much as she could before he arrived back. Because at that point, she got the feeling they might no longer speak freely.

At that moment, Dylan's phone rang again, and she saw his face change as he looked down.

"I'd better take this," he said, turning and walking out.

Grace felt a pang of anxiety. Whatever the number on the screen had been, it was clear that Dylan was expecting trouble to land.

CHAPTER SEVEN

"You see, I know who killed you. I know who it was."

The man spoke the words earnestly as he stared at the photo on the wall. His hands shook visibly as he lifted a hand to straighten the old, brass frame that housed the photo of the smiling blonde boy.

His hands had done that for a year now, and it was gradually worsening. He was used to the unsteadiness. It didn't bother him because when he needed them to be, his hands were extremely steady, and he had no problem with them.

But his mind... his mind was always racing, always calculating, always thinking. He couldn't escape it, even in his sleep. His nightmares were dark and torturous.

He was consumed by the constant need for answers, for justice, for revenge.

He took a step back to admire the photo, his gaze intense, and his mind racing.

"I know who killed you," he muttered.

The photo spoke back to him. It did that sometimes.

"I hope you find them," it said. He didn't see the lips actually moving, but even so, the words were clear. He liked it when the photo spoke to him, because it made him feel as if he'd scrolled back to a different time. A time when things were calmer and the world didn't feel so strangely tilted on its axis.

"It's a many headed hydra," he admitted. "And I'm cutting those heads off, one by one. There may be a few more. But I won't stop. I won't."

"Good!" the voice came back, and the man felt encouraged that he was on the right track.

Now, it was time to head out, because he was ready to take the next one.

He collected what he needed, dropping one of the items on the floor because of his hands. That was okay, they'd steady up when he needed them to.

He made his way to the car parked outside, his mind racing with the details of his next target. He knew it was risky, because he was going to have to take this target in twilight, before it was fully dark, but he couldn't let this evil person roam free any longer. He had to take action.

"Good afternoon." As he walked out of his house, he heard the greeting from the woman who lived opposite him.

"Afternoon," he nodded. He was able to seem normal when it mattered. He knew it was important to do that. He had to seem like an ordinary guy to others. He could not afford for them to sense his thoughts, because some of them might side with the agents of death.

This woman was elderly, with graying hair and spectacles. She owned a tiny white car that she drove at a crawl. She was one of the innocents - he hoped, at least. His research had not uncovered anything to contradict that.

"You going out then?" she asked, a pointless question, since he was headed to his car. She always asked the same question on the occasions when she saw him, and as always, he told her the same lie.

"Off for night shift now," he said. When he went out in the late afternoon or evening, he said it was night shift. She thought he was a shift worker, and that was boring and mundane enough that she'd never asked him more.

"Have a good day," she smiled, and he nodded back.

"You, too," he said, glad that the words sounded friendly, even though he was heading out on a mission of revenge, and relieved he'd maintained his cover with her, and the illusion of who she thought he was.

As he drove towards his destination, he felt the familiar rush of adrenaline. He knew that his hands would be steady now, and his mind would be sharp. It was time to face his next challenge.

He had to be careful driving. It wasn't as easy as it had been. The other cars didn't always stay in focus. Mostly they did but not always. Sometimes they flitted in and out of focus as if they were trying to evade him, and when they did that, he gave them a sharp, careful stare.

Because what if they were trying to evade him? He knew this conspiracy that the agents of death were organizing ran deep. He just didn't know how deep it ran and how much there would be for him to do.

There. This was where he was going. He'd scoped it out for days beforehand.

This target lived alone. Like the others. He could see why. When you were an agent of death, like they were, then there was no escaping your reality. People sensed it; he knew that. They picked it up, and would automatically try to avoid it.

He sensed it too. It was as if the evil emanated from them.

This was the humble house where she lived, the next target.

It was set in a rural area, an out-of-town setting. A little farmhouse on a larger piece of land, which had caused him some concerns, because would anyone from the farm see? Would any of the workers pass by? He knew this could be dangerous to him, because if he was caught, then he couldn't continue with his mission. His all-important and all-consuming task.

He'd checked out the house carefully, but unobtrusively, for a few days, being cautious, seen by nobody but the looming shadows that seemed to dance at the corners of his vision when he waited in the shade. That was okay. He didn't mind the shadows. They wouldn't go away, so he had come to think of them as innocent.

Now, he approached the home again, hoping his luck would hold and that today would be the same as yesterday, and the same as this day last week.

The house was small, with a quaint front garden. A white picket fence surrounded the property, making it seem idyllic. This target had little interest in gardening. That, he had observed. The grounds were maintained by people on the farm. That was what made them seem so well-intended and pleasant, as if a lovely and kind person dwelt within.

But he knew better. He knew that within the walls of that home lay a dangerous agent of evil. He felt his hands shaking again and clenched his fists to steady them.

No wonder she didn't like gardening. It was creating life, and she was a bringer of death. He thought about that with a sour sense of satisfaction as he huddled into the shade of the hedge.

Her car was parked outside the farmhouse, under a makeshift wooden shelter behind the hedge. So he was going to wait for her here.

It would happen quickly, he had no doubt about it. As he waited, as the time drew closer, he felt his thoughts focusing, just as he'd hoped they would.

She would come out of the house, and she would close the front door and lock it carefully. She would jingle her keys in her hand; that he knew. He'd heard her do it before. The jingling would get closer as she rounded the hedge.

Now he could see it in his mind; he could visualize it. Didn't they always say you had to visualize your goals? This was his goal and he could see it playing out now.

He'd have the gag ready. That took some preparation, and it was necessary to briefly stun his victims first. But not too much. He didn't want her completely unconscious when that gag went in.

He wanted her to know about it.

"You're going to know what you've done. Oh, yes, you'll know," he whispered.

Now he could feel the mists clearing and coherence returning to his thoughts. That sharp focus he needed was back again.

He felt grateful that the killing, this necessary task, seemed to summon what he required. His hands were totally steady as he crouched behind the hedge, and the mists that seemed to waft over his thoughts, seeping poison into them, had briefly cleared.

He waited patiently, his eyes fixed on the path that led to the cottage. He could hear the faint sounds of the farm in the distance, but they didn't distract him. He was too focused on his mission, too determined so nothing would get in his way.

Finally, he saw her coming out of the cottage, just as he had predicted. She locked the door and began to walk toward her car while jingling her keys. He could feel his heart racing as he prepared to make his move.

This was the last walk she would take. His muscles tensed. Her footsteps were close.

And now that walk was over.

CHAPTER EIGHT

"Tell me what you know about Thomas Lane," Grace invited the two secretaries. Now that Dylan had walked out to take the urgent phone call, she was alone with them and she sensed that they were gradually warming up to her, becoming more ready to talk. She hoped that she'd be able to get somewhere.

But, at that moment, she heard footsteps approach from outside. Not Dylan's footsteps. These were heavier and quicker, and both secretaries clearly recognized the sound.

They sat up in their chairs, automatically reached for their keyboards, and Bertha Evans straightened a pen on the desk.

The door opened, and Grace knew with a sinking of her heart that her chance had come and gone, because the boss was here.

"We've got an issue, because a key employee isn't in today," he began, his voice sharp. Then he saw Grace, and stopped abruptly, looking her up and down.

He was a balding man in his fifties, wearing a sharp gray suit and a stern expression. He had a prominent chin and deep-set eyes that turned to her with a mixture of curiosity and suspicion.

"FBI Agent Grace Ford," she introduced herself. "Are you Mr. Meyerson? I'm here in connection with Thomas Lane."

"Yes, I'm Meyerson. What's this about Thomas Lane?" he asked, his tone cold and guarded. "And what are you doing in here? We have very strict rules about these premises being accessed by outside visitors."

"I'm investigating his murder," Grace said.

"Look, it's a terrible thing. A terrible thing," Meyerson said, in tones that made it very clear he didn't think it was terrible, and that it was more of an inconvenience to him. "But what can it possibly have to do with his work? I mean, he clocked out as normal on Friday. I believe this happened sometime over the weekend and nobody really knows when or what took place? All I know is that he wasn't here for work on Monday."

Grace could sense Meyerson's defensiveness, and she knew that getting any information out of him would be like pulling teeth. She decided to try a different approach.

"Actually, Mr. Meyerson, I think Thomas Lane's murder might have something to do with work," she said, staring directly at him. "From what I understand, he had some kind of conflict or disagreement with a fellow worker?"

Meyerson's eyes narrowed, but he didn't deny it.

"I'm afraid I'm not authorized to speak about any disputes," he said, his tone clipped.

"What happened?" Grace asked. "What was the outcome?"

Meyerson shrugged. "We value our employees' privacy and we can't speak about issues that have been resolved. It wasn't a big problem in any case."

Both the secretaries nodded in unison.

"Was it a problem with one of the managers?" she asked.

Meyerson shook his head. "I'm not at liberty to speak about any interpersonal problems. Please understand, we can go no further with this. It's not my decision, it's company protocol that these issues are kept confidential." He folded his hands.

Grace knew that there were things he wasn't saying. He was giving her a rehearsed spiel and following a script. She glanced again at the secretaries, noticing that Bertha in particular was fidgeting.

That small sign of unease informed Grace that she knew about this, and was feeling bad that it wasn't being aired out now.

She decided that a subtle approach would work better than hardcore.

"Has Thomas Lane ever been in any other trouble?" she asked.

Meyerson shook his head. "No. I can tell you that he had a clear record. Very few instances of tardiness, no bad mistakes, and no big mishaps during his time in charge on the factory floor."

Grace nodded, taking in the information. "And what about his personal life? Did you ever find that interfering with work?"

Meyerson frowned. "I don't think so. We don't really pry into our employees' personal lives. We're only concerned with their work performance."

Grace pressed on. "Did Thomas Lane ever mention anyone who had a grudge against him or any strange occurrences?"

Now, Meyerson was starting to look impatient. "You're wasting my time with these questions," he said.

Grace was now annoyed with his evasiveness. “No, Mr. Meyerson. You’re wasting my time with unclear answers. That’s the truth of it! So from here, it changes. I’ve had enough of your evasion and your refusal to cooperate. We need the information you’re suppressing. A murder investigation is a far more serious issue than any company protocols. You have two choices. Answer me here, or my partner and I will bring all of you into the police station for a more intense interrogation.”

Now, both the secretaries were very quiet. In fact, the entire office was quiet, and the only thing that could be heard was the sound of Meyerson's breathing. He was looking at the floor, his face flushed.

“I’ll start by speaking to your secretaries individually for a few minutes. And then, I’ll need to speak to you." Firmly, Grace set out the protocols. She was sure that the secretaries in particular had more to tell her. She wanted to ask them about this situation. That was when the uneasiness and small fidgeting actions she'd noticed had started.

At that moment, the door opened and Dylan walked back in, pocketing his phone. They all glanced at him, and Grace had time to see that his face looked serious, and his eyes sharp and intent.

He'd discovered something, she thought. But there wasn't time to ask because Meyerson was still in full flood.

"Look, you can speak to the secretaries. But I have an extremely busy schedule today, and we have one key employee, Jim Penney, who's taken unauthorized leave, and I'm now having to fill in for him and plan ahead. And that's where we need to be now. Planning. Can I at least get that done while you speak to the secretaries?"

He gestured to the door, now looking appealing rather than obstructive.

Grace shook her head.

“I’m not willing to let you leave this office until we have answers,” she said.

And then, Dylan dropped the bombshell that shocked all of them.

"Sir," he said, "I'm FBI Agent Reed. Regarding Jim Penney, I've just been on the phone to my superior. And we got the news that the second body in this serial case has been identified. It's your employee, Mr. Penney himself. He's not taking unauthorized absence. He's been murdered. And this now points the finger squarely at Lewes Inc. Your company is going to be in the spotlight now, and for all of the wrong reasons."

Into the shocked silence, he added, "So I would suggest you cooperate. As of now."

CHAPTER NINE

Grace felt as shocked as Meyerson now looked. Dylan had dropped a bombshell that she knew had changed the direction of this case. Both victims worked for Lewes Inc.? This changed everything, and it broadened the field of suspects.

This might no longer be a personal issue related to Thomas Lane and his conflict with a manager. It might be something bigger.

"You do realize this changes everything, Mr. Meyerson," she said, after exchanging a quick raise of the eyebrows with Dylan. "You're obviously aware of the consequences that bad publicity could have for the company? And of course, you are going to want to keep your other employees safe, if people here are being targeted?"

Meyerson nodded stiffly, his face pale. He opened and shut his mouth a few times, grappling with this bombshell.

"You're sure about that?" he asked Dylan.

"Yes. The body was identified this morning, by Jim Penney's sister. I believe he was expected at a family dinner last night with her, and never arrived. She called in a missing person alert first thing this morning, and she's just been to identify his body."

That could have been matched up sooner. While she waited for Meyerson to come to terms with this blow, Grace realized that the delay was due to the police detective in charge. He was working slowly.

His demeanor came back into her mind again, and this time, she started to understand the truth. Detective Stoll, the gray-mustached lead investigator, was the one dragging his heels.

She didn't think Stoll was incompetent or corrupt. But she thought he was tired. The seriousness of this case was not a burden that this detective wanted to carry. It was exactly the same situation as her own previous partner in the FBI, Dale, had eventually faced.

Dale had ended up being injured in a car crash, and he was still on medical leave after a complicated leg break. When he returned to work, Grace was sure he would opt for a step down to a desk job. Stoll was in the same mindset. This was why the investigation was going slowly, and they needed to make up for Stoll's lack of motivation.

But a loud throat clearing from Meyerson drew her away from these thoughts, and back to the problems of her present situation.

"Okay. I see we do have a potential crisis here," Meyerson admitted.

"It's not a potential crisis, sir," Dylan corrected him. "It's a full blown crisis. It's landed, and now we just have to try to manage it as best we can. Could I speak to you in your office, now?"

Divide and conquer was definitely going to be the best way forward, and Grace felt pleased that Dylan had been perceptive enough to grasp the situation at a glance.

"Yes. I'll pull up the employee records and we can take a look," Meyerson capitulated. He headed through to the office beyond, with Dylan following. A moment later, the door closed.

Taking her chance, Grace pulled up a chair and sat down, choosing the desk where Bertha Evans sat, as she'd been the one who had shown most clearly that she knew something.

But just in case the other woman knew more, she made sure to direct her questions to both of them.

"I know you both must be very shaken up by this news, but it's important that we get as much information as we can. Did you know either of the two victims well? Or know if anything out of the ordinary was happening in their lives?"

The two women glanced at each other. Grace waited. She felt sure that they knew something. But it wasn't going to be easy to get the truth out of them.

"Nothing, really," the dark haired secretary said hesitantly.

"How long had Thomas been working for the company?" she asked, hoping to get a picture of who knew what, and what might have played out in the timeframe.

It was the gray-haired Bertha who responded.

"Look, I've been here seven years, Thomas joined a year or two later, and during my time I've seen a few things that we've been told not to talk about publicly," she said. "I really can’t say more than that. I’m only telling you this much because of these murders."

"It's frightening to think that someone is targeting employees here. I guess that includes us," the other secretary said.

"Did you hear about any incident involving either of these two men? Mr. Lane or Mr. Penney?" Grace pushed. “What was the conflict with the manager about? Is there anything else that you can tell me about either man?”

The two secretaries exchanged another glance before Bertha spoke up. "I heard some rumors, but I am not sure if they are true or not."

"Rumors?" Grace leaned forward. "What kind of rumors?"

"I did hear what you said, that Thomas and a few other employees had some kind of severe grievance with one of the managers a while ago," the gray-haired secretary admitted. "I don't know the details, but it sounded pretty serious. I believe the manager left soon afterward. He was in another department, so I don't know his name. They make it difficult to find out things like that. Gossip is discouraged here," she said softly.

Grace leaned in. "Do you know who the other employees were?"

The secretary shook her head. "I don't know. I just overheard some conversation in the break room."

And then, the other secretary spoke up. "I also heard whispers about something like that a while ago, but I thought that Mr. Penney was involved."

"Mr. Penney? Are you sure?" Grace asked.

The secretary nodded. "Yes, I'm positive. I remember hearing about it and thinking it was strange because he seemed like such an easygoing person, the couple of times I met him. He worked in a different department, so I didn't have that much to do with him. It's only now that it's coming back to me. But I don't know any of the details."

Grace felt a jolt of excitement. This was a strong lead. Had both these men trodden on the wrong toes? Had someone been fired, or asked to leave, and then gotten payback?

"Do you have any idea who the manager was?"

Both secretaries shook their heads. "I'm sorry, Agent. I don't know," Bertha said.

"Who would know?" Grace asked.

"Coworkers might know," Bertha said.

"And HR would know who left recently," the other secretary said. "But it's impossible to get that information from HR, especially if there were any problems. They don't like to share that kind of thing."

Grace nodded. She didn't rate her chances of getting the facts from HR easily, and suspected that they would be even worse than Meyerson in terms of unhelpfulness. Coworkers would be a better idea. Surely the others on the factory floor knew more?

This office window overlooked the factory building. It wouldn't be difficult to find her way there. And she decided she was going to do it now. Before Dylan finished up with Mr. Meyerson, and before Mr. Meyerson could decide it was now time for them to leave.

This company guarded its secrets closely, and she knew that there were secrets to be found.

Time to start digging. On her own, and fast.

"Thank you for your help," she said, standing up and quickly leaving the office.

As soon as she was out, she texted Dylan. *"I have a lead. Going down to the factory before they can try to warn anyone not to talk."*

Then, Grace headed downstairs and walked out of the reception building, heading along the walkway that led behind it, and trying to look as if she had every right to be there.

CHAPTER TEN

The walkway was made from roughened concrete, and looked to have been recently sluiced down. Shallow puddles still lay in the shade of the high walls that formed a corridor. Grace strode along it, looking businesslike and purposeful, hoping that when she rounded the corner, she'd find a way into the factory itself.

She was now hell bent on discovering what went on here.

The company that had previously been no more than a name for them to investigate, was now becoming an entity that felt more complex. It had a personality. It was a place where people clashed, where political moves were made, and where secretaries and managers were asked not to speak about anything.

And where HR was an impenetrable black hole when it came to getting details about people who'd left.

She guessed that since this was a chemical manufacturer that presumably held a lot of complex, confidential recipes, this was to be expected. But even so, as she rounded the corner, following wet footprints from other people who'd tracked through the puddles, she felt that there was a definite air of secrecy here.

Ahead was the factory door, and it was massive - about four yards wide, high enough to permit the biggest of trucks or tankers, and it was open. But as she peeked around, she saw an officious looking man, in black overalls with a notepad and an iPad, standing at the entrance.

This place was guarded. The black-clad man was busy signing someone in, and since he had his back to her, she peered around to see inside.

Immediately, she picked up the strong reek of chemicals. It was pungent, almost suffocating. She breathed slowly and tried not to cough. She didn't want to alert the guard while she got a picture of what was happening here.

The factory was busy. Machines whirred and hissed, and workers in yellow and green safety gear moved around, checking gauges and adjusting valves. Grace could hear the hum of conversation, but couldn't make out any individual words.

This wasn't a place where questions could be asked. That, she saw immediately. It was noisy, and everyone inside was extremely busy, moving to and fro amid the reeking fumes. Plus, the guard had a clear view of the factory floor and she'd stand out immediately even if she did sneak past him.

What about a break room? Grace was going to guess that there must be a break room nearby, probably adjacent to the restrooms. And if she managed to catch a few of the workers on their break, that would be the best chance she had to speak to them.

Where would such a room be located? Presumably outside the factory itself, because employees would have to clock out to go on their break. This seemed like the kind of place where hours would be strictly regulated.

So, left or right?

Deciding to try right, just because there seemed to be more space beyond the building in that direction, Grace turned that way and walked quickly along the factory building's outer wall, glad to be out of sight of that guard.

As she walked, she noticed that the pungent scent of chemicals was quickly fading. She guessed that the break room would be somewhere nearby. Time, after all, was money.

There was a small room at the far corner of the factory. That looked like a good place for a break room and a restroom.

Approaching it, she saw a door with a small window adjacent to it and peeked through. Inside was a small room, equipped with vending machines and a few tables and chairs. Her heart rate quickened as she saw a few workers sitting, taking a break and chatting. The walls were covered in official notices and a big No Smoking sign. It might be a break room, but it wasn't exactly a friendly environment.

Time to go in and see if she could find anything out.

Grace walked inside. There were three men sitting at a table and speaking in low voices. The acrid smell of cheap instant coffee filled the air. One of the men was eating some homemade food from a lunch box. Another was munching on a candy bar from the vending machine.

They all turned when she walked in and looked at her in shock.

Dressed in factory overalls, the men looked to be in their mid to late twenties. That was around Thomas's age, so she felt encouraged that they might have been friendly with him.

"I'm Agent Grace Ford, FBI," she said, showing her badge. "I'm here to get information on the recent crimes involving two workers at Lewes Inc."

They knew about Thomas. That was clear. She was wondering if that was exactly the conversation they'd just been having in low voices. But as her words hit home, she saw that they definitely did not know there had been a second murder.

"Two? I'm sorry, ma'am, we don't know anything about that. All we know is that Tom Lane was murdered. I'm not sure we should be talking to you. We have very strict rules, and this is a prohibited area to visitors."

The closest man spoke the words, frowning worriedly. He was a tall, long-limbed man with blonde hair cut short, and blue eyes set close together, giving him a focused look.

"Who are you?" Grace asked him.

"I'm Daniel," he said. "I worked with Tom here. And these are my colleagues, Jake and Mark."

Grace nodded at them, taking in their expressions. She could see that they were all wary, and understandably so. They didn't expect to be confronted by a rogue FBI agent, breaking company rules, while on their break.

"Who's the other person who's been killed?" Jake - a shorter man with a head of unruly looking dark hair - asked, fidgeting nervously with his coffee spoon.

No reason not to say, she thought.

"The other victim was IDed this morning, and he's Jim Penney," she said.

Two of them - Jake and Mark - looked blank, but Daniel's eyes widened.

"I know Tom was friends with Jim, although I didn't know him myself, as he worked in a different department," he said. "What on earth's going on?"

"That's exactly what we're trying to find out," Grace said. "Did Tom talk about any trouble recently? I understand there was an issue involving a manager?"

The men stared at each other. She watched them. Unspoken communication was happening here. The problem was that she needed spoken communication. Why was everyone at Lewes Inc. being so cagey?

"Look, anything you say will remain confidential," Grace said.

Still more silence. She wasn't getting through to them and she knew the clock was ticking. The lunch box was empty, the candy wrapper was crumpled. Just now, these men were going to excuse themselves and flee back to the factory to restart their shifts.

She needed to try a more persuasive angle and she had one. But it was the last in her toolbox. If this didn't work, nothing would.

"You do realize that this crime, and the killer’s modus operandi, puts all of you at risk?" she said.

That jolted them.

"What do you mean?" Daniel asked, his voice hoarse with concern.

"I mean that whoever is behind these murders is still out there. We don't know how the victims are chosen, but it seems they're taken after hours. While he’s at large, everyone here is in danger. All of you. And if you have any information that could help us catch the killer, it's in your best interest to come forward," Grace explained, hoping the fear in their eyes would push them to talk.

"It's better to say something," Mark muttered.

"You sure it will be confidential?" Daniel asked.

"Yes, it will. I won't say who told me," Grace promised.

Daniel ran a hand through his hair, his brow furrowed in thought. "Yeah, there was some tension between Tom and one of the managers here, and it peaked during the summer. I think a few of the guys started getting angry about it. The manager was a guy named Alex Stratton. He was always riding Tom and the others hard, pushing them to work longer hours and get more done. Tom was a good worker, but he was starting to get pretty stressed out by it."

"He was abusive, too. I mean, really foul-mouthed," Jake added.

"Tom and a few others eventually went and spoke to senior management about it," Dale said. "I think Jim was one of that group, too, because he also worked directly under Alex. They complained about it, and HR got to hear about it, and the next thing, Alex was told to leave. Fired, basically."

"But Tom had to sign a non-disclosure agreement," Mark said. “He told us that and said it was why he couldn’t say anything more, or he’d be fired, too.”

"Yes, that's right. It was all hushed up big time. The manager left and then it was like the whole situation was just erased."

Grace nodded. "This is very helpful. I appreciate what you've told me," she said.

It had taken time, and some trespassing, but eventually she'd gotten to the truth about Tom's problematic relationship in the company. And it now looked to be an extremely promising lead.

As the three men got up and rushed out of the break room, Grace made her way back to the main entrance in just as much of a hurry.

She needed to update Dylan on what she'd found.

And then, they both needed to track down Alex Stratton, an ex-manager with a clear motive for revenge.

CHAPTER ELEVEN

Grace hustled back to the car, hoping that Dylan would already be there. She was in luck. He was waiting inside.

She swung open the door and got in.

"I got a lead from some of the coworkers," she said. "I found out who the manager was that Thomas, and also Jim, were in conflict with. He got fired, or at any rate, he was forced to leave. His name's Alex Stratton."

"You got all that?" His eyebrows rose. "Well done."

"Did you get anything?" she asked, already busy opening her laptop and logging into the police databases to find Alex's address.

He shook his head. "Not a thing. I didn't get as much as a hint from Meyerson. And I reckon he was schooled in evasion. Those answers were just running rings around me."

"And you kept trying?" she asked.

Dylan made a wry face. "To be honest? I was listening in on the outside. I thought you might have gotten onto a line of inquiry outside, and then I heard the door close, so I thought you were heading somewhere."

"You did?" Grace asked, surprised again by his perception.

"Yeah. And then your message came through. I reckoned if Meyerson got out of his office, he'd ask the secretaries what they'd said, and try to block you, so I kept him talking about nothing. Asked him about his career, that kind of thing. General topics, you know? Then when I couldn't think of anything else to say, I finally left. I got to the car two minutes ago."

"You did a damned good job there," Grace praised. She couldn't believe how perceptive Dylan had been. He seemed able to think four moves ahead, and she realized that she had a lot to learn from this creative man she'd been partnered with. "Because I did go somewhere else. I went to the factory."

"And what did you find?"

"It was toxic." She wrinkled her nose at the memory. "Horrible place. And there was another guard at the entrance. I avoided him and found the break room."

"You did that? Good move." Dylan looked admiring too.

"I talked to a couple of people who knew Thomas, and they mentioned this conflict with a manager."

She glanced down at the screen. She was in, and she'd found Alex Stratton. Now, she just had to look for his address.

"Why were they in conflict?" Dylan asked.

"He was apparently abusive to Tom and Jim, and there was big tension between them. They escalated it, and he got fired. But Tom and everyone else involved had to sign a non-disclosure agreement."

"Being fired is a big motive for revenge," Dylan said, nodding. "Let's go pay him a visit."

Finally, there was a way forward, and Grace felt relieved. "I have the address here," she said. "It's in Northlands, a town about twenty minutes from here." She searched some more, this time looking into his social media profile. "You know what I don't have?"

"What's that?" he asked.

"I don't have any record of a new employer. I'm guessing he's still unemployed?"

Now, her mind was being filled with ideas of a man with a grudge, a man who wanted payback.

Dylan started the car and they drove off. Grace inputted the address into the GPS, glad to get on the road and to turn her back on the chemical manufacturing company. There had been something creepy about it. All her instincts had been prickling in there.

As they drove, Grace started to think about what they would say to Alex when they arrived. She wondered if he would even talk to them readily. After all, he might also have signed non-disclosure agreements, and they might need to pressure him.

"I think we should prepare a search warrant in case we need one," she said. "It might take some time to organize, and there's a chance we'll need it." Her mind was on that evidence again. Those gags, those chemicals.

"You think?" Dylan quirked an eyebrow at her again.

"I'm trying to be prepared, and prevent delays," she protested.

"I disagree. I think we go ahead and question him without one," Dylan pointed out. "If he's guilty, we might have probable cause to search his place without needing that."

"So you're suggesting we wing it?" She felt horrified by the thought.

He narrowed his eyes. "Particularly if we suspect something and push his buttons."

"So then we'll have reason to search?"

"Exactly," he said.

She felt more doubtful, but then again, she also wasn't familiar with this part of the US and the way the local people behaved, and he was. If he thought a situation was going to play out in a certain way, then all she could do was go along with it.

It didn't come easy to her, and she realized with surprise that she really did feel out of her depth in this area.

It was not the way an FBI agent was supposed to feel. She'd excelled at her job, but now, she was asking herself all over again - had she been stagnating without realizing it? Had this decision to join the Mississippi task force been something that had redeemed her career?

As they drove down the quiet suburban streets of Northlands, a neat suburb that got more and more pristine the further they drove through it, Grace wondered what they'd find when they arrived at Alex Stratton's house.

"Nice neighborhood," Dylan commented. He was also gazing from side to side and taking in the well ordered homes that were located on progressively larger lots, the ornate yards, the privacy fencing, the large parks, and the strip malls with fashion boutiques and good restaurants.

They arrived at Alex Stratton's house, a two-story brick home that was set far back from the street. The yard was immaculately landscaped, and there was a large fountain in the front, trickling water gently over its stone borders.

In Minnesota, that fountain would have frozen over by now, Grace acknowledged, climbing out and heading up to the front door. She hadn't expected Alex Stratton, fired - or at any rate dismissed - from Lewes Inc., to live in such luxurious surrounds. She had questions.

Hopefully, once she hammered on that front door, she'd get some answers.

She knocked, and waited, glancing at Dylan, who had his head raised, admiring the upstairs balcony. Or else, maybe, looking for any movement from behind those tinted French doors.

And then, she heard footsteps approach.

The door creaked open, revealing a man in his mid-thirties with dark hair cut in an edgy style, faded at the sides, and a toned physique. His eyes, a deep blue, narrowed as he stared at them.

He was wearing a designer golf shirt in burgundy, with a jacket slung over it. The fact that he was standing on a Persian carpet below a hallway chandelier cemented in Grace's mind that this man was not battling financially.

"FBI," she said. "Alex Stratton? We have a few questions."

"Oh," he said, doing a double take to see them on the doorstep. He'd clearly been expecting other company, she realized, probably golf related.

His face changed. "I don't think so," he shot at them. With reactions that were speedier than she'd anticipated, he slammed the door in their faces.

CHAPTER TWELVE

Grace had a moment to think despairingly that she'd been right, that they should have gotten a warrant, because this was all over now.

Only Alex Stratton didn't get his front door closed. Dylan, with reactions that were far quicker than she believed possible, shoved his foot in the way.

Alex made a desperate attempt to slam it again, but it was too late. The heavy door bounced off the side of Dylan's boot, and then Dylan grabbed the handle, forcing it open.

"Answers please, sir! Now!" he said.

Grace clearly picked up the rage in Alex's face. For sure, this suspect had something to hide.

"This is my private residence," he bellowed, but face-to-face with them, and an open door between them, there was little he could do.

"First question. Are you Alex Stratton?" Grace asked the dark-haired man, needing to confirm his identity. He was still clinging onto the door handle, pressing all his weight against it, but now looking much less sure of himself as he stared down at her badge.

"Yes, I am. And I already told you, I don't have anything to say," he snapped. He tried again to close the door, flinging his entire body weight suddenly against it, but Dylan was ready for him, returning the pressure, keeping his foot wedged in and his shoulder firmly against the door.

Now, Alex's face was flushed with anger. He was mad that he wasn't able to dislodge them from his doorstep.

"We're investigating a series of murders. We need information," Dylan said. He was physically on guard, his muscles taut, clearly not trusting Alex an inch. That was fine. She didn't either.

Alex's eyes flickered with a hint of doubt, but he quickly masked it with arrogance. "I don't know anything about any murders. You're wasting your time here."

"We have heard that you had contact with both victims," Grace said.

Alex wrinkled up his face in a parody of disbelief.

"You can't be serious. You come here and plant yourselves on my front doorstep, telling me that I somehow spoke to two murder victims before they died? I don't even know who they are!"

That last sentence was a little too loud, a little too defensive. Grace guessed he had a very good idea who they were.

"They're Thomas Lane and Jim Penney," she said. "Both worked for the company you left a few months ago."

He raised his chin again. "I'm sorry, of course. But I have nothing to say."

Dylan shrugged. "That's a pity," he said.

"Why's that?" Alex asked.

"Because there's clear evidence linking you to the victims. Multiple witnesses have mentioned it. So, if you keep denying it, we'll have to take you in for questioning. And if we find any evidence that links you to the murders, we'll have to arrest you. Ever spent a night in jail? It'll be very different from your nice house here," Dylan threatened.

Alex's façade crumbled slightly at that, and he hesitated. "I...I don't know what you want to hear," he stammered.

"Letting us in would be a good start," Grace said.

"We can always talk at the police station, if you don't want us to come in," Dylan added meaningfully.

Finally, Alex was starting to capitulate, and Grace saw him realize that they were not just going to go away.

"Fine," he said, stepping aside reluctantly. "Come in."

Once they were inside, Alex led them to a luxurious living room, complete with plush, white leather sofas and a large fireplace. Grace looked around curiously, seeing that there were several objects and photos on the wall that showed Alex was a keen traveler. An African mask, a Japanese screen, a few magnums of French champagne.

As for the man himself, he was staring at them with an uneasy defiance.

"Listen, I don't have to answer your questions," he said. "I let you in because you refused to leave. But I know my rights."

Grace nodded. "You have the right to a lawyer, of course. But if you're innocent, you shouldn't need one. And you do have to answer our questions. We're law enforcement officers, investigating a murder case. Refusal to answer is a criminal offense."

He stared at her, his gaze dark. "You think I don't know that?"

"Why are you being evasive and uncooperative then?" Grace pressured him.

"You don't know it, but I'm treading a fine line here," he said.

Grace and Dylan exchanged glances. Grace was curious now. She thought that the threat of jail had jolted Alex out of his arrogance, and that they might finally now get the truth from him. She was curious to know what it would be.

"What do you mean by that?" she asked.

"I mean that I can answer your questions, but get myself into a whole heap of different trouble," he said.

Grace shrugged. "We don't want to cause trouble. We just want to know your involvement with the victims, and if you have any information on the murders. That's it," she said.

He was silent for a while. Then, he took a deep breath.

"Look, those workers conspired to get me out," he blustered. "That work environment, it wasn't an easy place. Being a manager there was tough."

"Okay?" Grace said.

"If you tried to do things according to company protocols, you were accused of being a bully. Protocols were strict. I followed them. I ended up between a rock and a hard place. Then the team I'd been managing turned on me. And yes, both those men you mentioned were a part of it. Thomas was one of the ringleaders."

"And they forced you to leave?"

"The directors said it was impossible for me to stay," he agreed.

Grace looked again around the beautifully decorated living room.

"How did it make you feel, being out of a job?" she asked.

He was silent a while longer.

"I get what you're hinting at," he then shot out. "You're trying to insinuate that I was bankrupt and I killed them as payback. Well, it wasn't like that. The truth was that I was in senior management there, and I also have a very good lawyer. Plus, I had insider knowledge of a lot of processes and recipes. My lawyer fought for me, and the company agreed that I would keep their trademarked information highly confidential in return for a very good payout."

"Is that so?"

He shrugged. "I knew a lot. All my experience hinged on what I knew. For me to have gone elsewhere would be pretty much impossible. So yes, I got an early retirement package, you might say. I know important information, trademarked recipes, and I have client details that are kept confidential. So they made sure I'd never need to work again. In fact, it was the best thing that could have happened to me."

He gave a tight smile. "But I suppose you're going to try and tell me that this all sounds a bit too convenient, right?"

Grace actually thought the answer made sense, but Dylan was drumming his fingers thoughtfully on the leather couch, as if considering that exact question for himself.

"I believe that your version could be legitimate," Grace said, and she genuinely did think so. She had a feeling that if they tried to find out anything more about the company's practices, they would be coming up against that lawyer immediately. Alex meant what he said. He was keeping his mouth shut in exchange for a clearly generous sum of money.

That raised many more questions for her about what went on at Lewes Inc., but those were questions for another day. Right now, she needed to confirm his whereabouts.

"Can you account for your time over the weekend?" she asked. "And how about last night?"

The problem was that the timeframes for when the victims had been taken were very broad. She doubted that he could account for his time. But, surprisingly, she was wrong.

"On the weekend, I was away," he said.

"Where?" Dylan asked.

"I was on a golfing tour with three of my friends. We flew down to Palm Beach on Thursday night, and got back Monday afternoon. We played three different courses on Friday, Saturday and Sunday. You want confirmation? I can give it to you."

Grace nodded. "Please," she said.

A confirmed alibi was a surprise twist she'd never expected to find when she arrived here. But her suspicions were now even more sharply focused on Lewes Inc.

As Alex took his phone and began scrolling through to find the necessary proof, Grace's phone began ringing.

It was Tyler. She felt a jolt of unwelcome surprise as she saw his number on the screen.

"Can you check the details?" she asked Dylan. "I need to take this."

Quickly, Grace strode out of Alex's mini-mansion, to take the call in the front yard, surprised and taken aback by the emotion she'd felt as she'd seen his number on the screen.

She had no idea whether he was calling because there was a problem back home, or else just to wish her a friendly goodnight.

But she worried it was to continue the fight.

CHAPTER THIRTEEN

What had happened?

She felt groggy and disoriented, as if she'd had a really high fever or a terrible hangover. Her mouth tasted foul, as if poisons were lodged in her throat. Her lungs burned, and mists swirled around her. She had the impression they were more inside her head than out of it.

What on earth was the rattling and banging that threatened to split her head apart?

It wasn't just a noise. She was being painfully banged about, and as she slowly focused, she realized that she was in a truck.

In the back of a truck. She could see the windows above her.

But she couldn't move. Her hands were tied. And she couldn't breathe, because there was something soft, squashy, and damp in her mouth, pressing down on her tongue. That was causing the vile taste. It felt as if poisons were leaking from it. It was bitter and repellent and it made her want to throw up.

She tried to breathe, now terrified, panicking. Her stomach churned and hitched, and she desperately tried to suppress that reflex. Throwing up now would be a bad, bad idea. It would kill her, because she wouldn't be able to dislodge whatever the heck was in her mouth.

She'd left the house to drive to the neighborhood social, as she did the same time every week. She'd left the house, and had been heading for the car, but she hadn't made it there. What had happened? Something had banged down on the back of her head. She remembered that, but not much else.

Who had done this to her? And why? She struggled to figure it out, but her thoughts were still muddled, and her vision was blurry. The banging and jolting of the ride was disorienting, and she feared with a terrible sense of inevitability that when it stopped, things would only get worse.

As if her own thoughts had predicted its movements, the truck jolted to a stop, and she heard the driver get out. Panic surged within her, and she twisted and turned, trying to free herself from the ropes that bound her.

The door opened, and a man stepped inside. He was wearing a mask, and his eyes glinted with malice as he looked down at her.

Then, with arms that seemed insanely strong, he scooped her up.

That action caused a wave of dizziness and she half lost consciousness again, only vaguely aware of being carried. The mists swirled and loomed.

And then, he was gone, and she was lying somewhere cold. Very cold. Her hair felt as if it was floating. Her body was half buried. If only she wasn't so weak. She knew she needed to struggle, that she had to fight to save her life, but she couldn't move.

Blearily, she tried to make sense of what was happening. Was she buried alive? It was so dark.

As she lay there, trying to push through the haze clouding her thoughts, her eyes slowly began to adjust to the darkness. She could faintly make out the outline of her captor standing in front of her.

Then she heard a voice. A weird, disembodied sounding voice, which was coming and going together with her fading thoughts.

"This is what you deserve; you brought it upon yourself. You know why this is happening, don't you? Don't you? I shouldn't have to tell you this! You should know it for yourself. It's your punishment. You get yours, just as you caused mine. You caused my pain and you will pay!"

The words were like an endless diatribe, although she didn't know how much of it was real and how much of it was replaying in her own confused mind. Why did she feel so ill? What had happened?

Could this be anything to do with her ex-partner? Was it him?

That thought flashed briefly into her mind, as a moment of clarity pierced the terror. That business partner had made a mess of things. And she'd taken her eye off the ball for a while to try and develop the other side of the business, which dealt with the manufacture of products. That had taken her into town all day, most days, and she hadn't focused on what was happening back at the ranch, so to speak.

But since they'd gone their separate ways, she had been trying to clean the mess up. And, she thought, succeeding in her task. It was much better than it had been; the crisis was over.

And yet, still, the tendrils of her thoughts were grasping at that concept, unwilling to leave it alone, and she realized that it must have some strange connection with the nonstop haranguing that her clouded mind was hearing off and on.

She tried to focus on that connection, but the mists were thronging again, her mind was too muddled, and the voice continued to taunt her. She felt a wave of fear wash over her as the reality of her situation hit her full force. She was trapped, alone, and at the mercy of whoever had done this to her.

If only she could plead with this man, or tell him that she had no idea what was happening and she was most likely innocent of whatever he was accusing her of. Most probably it was her partner that he'd meant to grab, but he was gone. Long gone. She was on her own now. Fixing things.

Or was she? The fuzziness in her head made it difficult to tell what was happening.

If only she could think! Why did she feel so disoriented, so weak?

Suddenly, a cold breeze rushed over her, causing her to shiver uncontrollably. She wanted to gasp at the shock of it, but the vile substance in her mouth choked her.

And then, too late, she realized.

It wasn't a breeze.

It was water. Cold water, lapping at her body. Water, from a river rising, that was now flooding over her, touching her chin, her face, soaking the gag anew, sending the poison trickling down her throat, as the water rushed into her nose, her eyes.

She tried to struggle, tried to fight it, but the mists were thicker now.

At least the water had muffled the man's voice, or maybe he was gone.

He'd left her here, alone, to her fate, and as the water swelled and rose around her, she understood that this was the end.

CHAPTER FOURTEEN

"Tyler? What's up?" Grace asked, as soon as she was out of earshot of their former suspect. Standing out in the breeze, with clouds gathering overhead and blotting out the sunset, she acknowledged the weather matched her mood.

Her thoughts were now veering in the direction of a problem or disaster. The water heater had been an issue in the past. If it had stopped working, then she had the number for the technician who could fix it fast and cheaply. Mundane as this was, it might be necessary. And if she was going to be spending a week or two a month out of state, she needed to be prepared to sort out these issues.

"Grace. I just got home from work and wanted to check in with you," Tyler said.

"Thanks," she said. So it was a friendly goodnight. That was a huge relief. There was no emergency to deal with, and no continuation of the fight. Quickly, she updated him. "We're making some progress, and we're narrowing down that both the victims were employed by the same company. That gives us a direction to go in."

She couldn't say more, not when she was currently busy with the investigation, but she felt surprisingly touched that Tyler had thought to ask. That he cared enough to do that. It meant a lot, and it reassured her that there was a future for them, with her in this new role.

But she soon realized she was wrong.

"Well, that's good," he said.

"Thanks," she replied. She took a breath, ready to ask him about his day, but before she could, he spoke again.

"And when are you going to be home?"

"That, I don't know," she admitted.

"Are you going to spend tonight in Arkansas? How about tomorrow night? What's your timeframe? I mean, I deserve to know, don't I?" he pressured.

Grace scowled.

She'd interpreted his question wrongly. And now, this call was heading rapidly downhill. She was feeling angry about it. Here she was in the middle of a murder investigation where victims had been killed in the most brutal way, and Tyler, safe and warm and well-fed at home, was making it all about himself?

"I'm not sure, Tyler," she said, trying to keep the anger from seeping into her voice. "It depends on how the investigation goes. You know I can't just drop everything and come home. I have a job to do."

"Well, can't you give me an estimate? I need to know when to expect you back." There was a note in his voice she didn't like at all. It was a tone she hadn't picked up in the past, but she recognized it. A bullying tone. He was calling to harass her. That was the purpose of this call.

"I'll let you know as soon as I can," she said, now feeling furious, but also determined to keep her emotions in check. She didn't want Tyler to have the satisfaction of knowing that he'd gotten under her skin.

He sighed. "You could at least have called to update me, you know. I'm beginning to wonder if you really care."

"Tyler, right now, I've just wrapped up interviewing a suspect. I've got a ton of work left to do. I don't know when, or if, I'll get to sleep tonight."

"Look, I didn't know that!"

"These trips are hard work. Stressful and painful. I've been looking forward to messaging you when I was finally in bed. But I don't think it's acceptable for you to demand a phone call when I'm looking into the identity of a killer!"

She hadn't meant her words to sound so cutting. Maybe that was a side of her that he hadn't seen before. At any rate, there was an astounded silence. Then, sounding thoroughly miffed, he snapped back at her.

"Fine. Do what you want," he said before hanging up abruptly.

Grace stood there in the front yard, phone still pressed to her ear. A gust of wind whipped her hair into her face, but she didn't bother to brush it away.

What was happening to their relationship? Why was Tyler so clingy and demanding?

She had a job to do, and she couldn't just drop everything to rush home. And he knew that.

But he was being selfish and unreasonable, and she didn't know how to handle it. Worse still, she didn't know if she wanted to handle it. She was wondering, now that she had some distance from him, whether there was actually a future for herself and Tyler as a couple, because at this moment it didn't feel likely.

Dylan walked out, pocketing his phone and putting his notebook back in his laptop bag.

"Well, that was a good lead," he said. “Maybe we need to look in a similar direction. I guess we have to go and speak to Jim Penney's family now."

That was the next step. The two men could have connected outside of work; perhaps they had frequented the same bars, or known the same people.

Then, Dylan saw her face.

"Are you okay?" he asked. "You seem upset. Is anything wrong?"

Grace took a deep breath to try and calm the turmoil inside her. "It's nothing," she said unconvincingly. "Just a personal issue."

"You want to talk about it?" he asked as they got into the car.

Grace shook her head. "Thanks for the offer," she said. “But it won't help to talk. I think I’d say the wrong thing right now. It's something I need to figure out for myself.”

“That’s not always easy,” he said, and she heard real sympathy in the words which touched her.

“It’s not. But I’m not letting it affect our work. Or my mood, hopefully,” she said, giving him a reluctant, forced smile and trying to shove her irritation with Tyler all the way to the back of her mind. “Now, let's go speak to Penney's family, and see if we can get any further with this." She took a breath, wondering what else she could do that might possibly help them with this case.

“I don’t know if Stoll’s already got it in place, but if not, let’s call him on the way and ask if the police can patrol tonight, on both sides of the river, and look at all the vehicle entry points. At best, we might catch him. At worst, the police presence might be a deterrent.

With her mind now fully back on the case, she picked up her phone to make the call.

*

It was fully dark by the time they arrived at the home of Jim Penney's sister, Vicky Penney, who was the closest family member geographically to where he lived. Jim and his sister lived on opposite sides of a newly built housing estate on the eastern border of Jonesboro.

The house was a small, unassuming, single-story building in a row of identical homes. The yard was nothing more than a strip of mowed grass, and there was a blue painted swing outside.

Grace knew that the sister would still be experiencing the shock of hearing her brother had been murdered. The timing was far from ideal, but then, there was no such thing as good timing when it came to asking questions about violent death.

She got out of the car and walked up to the house, side by side with Dylan. The porch light was on, and Grace could make out the silhouette of a woman through the frosted glass of the front door. She looked to be speaking on the phone.

Grace waited a moment, hoping the sister would finish her call. Then, she tapped softly on the door.

Footsteps approached.

"Who's there?" the sister asked. Her voice was hoarse and sounded exhausted.

"FBI," Grace replied. “We'd like to ask you a few questions regarding your brother."

The door opened a few inches and Vicky Penney peered cautiously out. She was a plump woman with porcelain skin and rich brown hair, and Grace guessed that in better times her face would be cheerful. Now, it was drawn in concern.

Behind her, a young boy of about six, with the identical color hair, peeked around her.

"I know it's not a good time," Grace acknowledged. "I’m so sorry this has happened. Do you feel able to answer a couple of questions?"

Vicky glanced down at the boy, obviously not wanting to speak in front of him.

"Samuel, go to your room, honey. I'll be just a minute," she said. Then, she stepped outside, joining them on the porch and closing the door.

"This has been a terrible shock," she said. "I'm trying to keep things together, to fix dinner, to get my head around it all. I don't know how much help I can be."

Grace nodded sympathetically. "We understand how difficult this must be for you. We'll try to make this as quick as possible."

Vicky's eyes filled with tears. "I just can't believe it. Jim was such a good man, and there’s no way he deserved anything like this."

"Did you know him well?" Grace asked.

"Yes. We were quite close, and living nearby, we used to have dinner every few days. So yes, I knew what was going on in his life."

"Were there any problems with his work?" Grace asked.

Vicky looked at her blankly. "No, not that I know of. He didn't particularly like his work, but he was one of those guys who was always grateful for what they had. Better a monthly salary than no job at all, he used to say."

"Why didn't he like his work?" Dylan asked.

"He disliked the chemical side of things, and he was sure that he'd developed allergies from working in that environment. But then again, I have allergies and I work as a doctor's receptionist. So it might not have been caused by that, but instead a result of a family weakness," Vicky explained.

Grace took that in, noting that the toxic atmosphere might be impacting the employees.

"Did your brother ever mention a man called Thomas Lane?" Dylan asked Vicky.

She frowned. "He definitely mentioned Thomas a few times. He was a coworker, and they were friendly, but I don't think they socialized together."

"Any conflicts with anyone else?" Grace asked.

She shook her head again. "He wasn't that type of man. He never fought with anyone. He was a real people person, and a gentleman. I think it must have been a random crime. He used to go walking at night - there's a big park near here with a river running through it, and he could easily have been grabbed by the wrong person then."

"It's possible," Grace said, even though she didn't think so.

Apart from more focus on the chemical nature of the business both men had worked for, there seemed to be no further leads. Jim Penney hadn't been a troublemaker or a fighter. And he hadn't even known Thomas that well.

It seemed as if they were up against a dead end here.

But, as they thanked Vicky for her time, Grace's phone rang.

It was Detective Stoll calling, and she picked it up quickly, hoping that more evidence had come in, or that someone had come forward with information.

But the call wasn't good news. In fact, it was a bombshell.

"Agent Ford?" he said. "There's been another body found."

CHAPTER FIFTEEN

"Another body?"

Grace glanced at Dylan as they hustled to the car. He sounded as grim as she felt. This case wasn't getting solved. They were hitting dead end after dead end, and the killer was rampaging ahead.

"Yes," she said. "Detective Stoll is sending us the coordinates now."

As Dylan started the car, the message came through.

The site was about twenty miles due east, on the river bank, but looking at the coordinates, Grace saw that this time the body had been dumped on the other side of the state line.

"This body is in Tennessee," she said, reading Stoll's message. "They've just realized it's a Tennessee jurisdiction."

Immediately, she saw the complications that would ensue. This was exactly why the task force had been formed, so that the resulting jurisdictional issues could be overcome. Stoll himself was not technically in control of this crime scene, and she guessed that the Tennessee police might end up managing the situation.

All they could do was get there, as fast as possible, and hope that this time the killer had left a clue behind.

As they sped toward the river, Grace stared out of the window, taking in this new development and its implications. This killer was crossing state lines now. She didn't know if that was deliberately done, to make things more difficult. And she also didn't know how old this body was. It might be a few days old, or a week or more.

Either way, a third victim was a massive escalation in this case. And, if the victim was recent, then he was shortening his killing interval.

When they arrived, they were met with a chaotic scene. Stoll was handing over to the Tennessee police, and police from both Arkansas and Tennessee were trying to secure the area, but the river site was close to a small town, and it seemed as if the entire population had turned up to stare in concern at the grisly sight. The roadside was lined with crowds, and knots of people were standing by, swathed in jackets and shining flashlights at the scene. Questions were being asked in loud, concerned voices.

“What happened here?”

“Is this another one of those murders, like what’s been happening in Arkansas?”

“How are you going to keep us safe?”

Detective Stoll, who seemed to be wrapping up his activity on the scene, saw Grace and Dylan approaching. He hurried to meet them and escorted them past the police cordon, and down the muddy river park.

"The victim is a woman," he muttered, as soon as they were out of earshot of the public.

Grace felt her heart sink. A woman? This was a departure from the pattern.

They navigated the slippery, muddy pathway down toward the scene, where spotlights were now glaring, and the body was visible, half buried in the mud.

"Do we have an ID for this victim?" This was her first and most important question to Stoll. Was this a third employee of Lewes Inc., as she suspected?

"Not yet. No ID on her," Stoll explained with a shake of his head.

"Who found her?" Grace then asked.

"Police from the Arkansas and Tennessee departments were patrolling the river on both sides of the state line," Stoll explained. "As per your advice, and my instructions. One of the first police patrols to go out came down here to check. As you can see, it's a popular fishing spot, and there's a road leading almost all the way down to the river."

"Any footprints?"

Stoll shook his head. "The ground was too muddy and trodden to hold any prints. By the time the police patrol saw the body, they'd already walked over the path themselves."

Grace nodded, acknowledging the limitations. Police couldn't conduct routine patrols without treading on the pathways themselves, and wouldn't have seen the body until they had been almost all the way down to the river.

"We're lucky they found it," she said. "Is there an estimated time of death?" This question was asked to the coroner who was already on the scene and working on the woman's body.

He glanced up, this movement allowing Grace her first sight of the corpse's mud-streaked face. There was a gag in her mouth that looked identical to the others, and which was saturated with mud. Her eyes, staring up under the harsh lights, were blue, and her hair, although dark with water and mud, was probably blonde.

"She's been dead only a couple of hours," the coroner concluded. “Not more than three hours, I would guess, given her body temperature in this water.”

"Approximate age?" Grace asked.

"In her forties, or early fifties, most likely," he said.

So, a forty- or fifty-something woman, with blonde hair and blue eyes. Even at a company as large as Lewes Inc., Grace felt sure that they could narrow down whether this woman had worked for them. But not now. Now, it was already after nine p.m. and the chances of contacting HR were minimal.

With a fresh body on the scene, there was nothing they could do. They were in the frustrating position of having no real leads.

"Will you let us know if any missing persons reports are called in?" Grace asked Detective Stoll, who nodded.

"I'll contact you immediately if we hear of anything," he promised. “I’ve handed over now, and the Tennessee police will take it from here.”

Grace then went over to the Tennessee detective who was working at the scene. She asked him the same question, and took his phone number, giving him her card. She didn't want the confusion over state jurisdictions to cause any delay in finding the ID for this latest victim.

With that done, Grace turned to Dylan. Her adrenaline was still surging as it always did when she was at an active scene, but there was nowhere for it to be channeled.

“There must be some sign of where she was dumped?”

Given that they couldn’t get hold of Lewes Inc. until morning, at least this was a way of possibly picking up on some valuable trace evidence.

With flashlights in hand, putting on their foot and head covers, Grace and Dylan joined in the forensic search, combing the river paths, peering carefully into the muddy banks, looking for any sign or trace of a footprint, or a car tire track. Grace checked the river area, and then walked up to the road, searching there too. She worked for the better part of an hour with Dylan, until the hope she’d had that there might be evidence in this fresh crime scene gradually curdled into resignation that it wasn’t offering them anything.

"I don't know what else we can do tonight," she said. “There’s no trace to be found, and there are no other leads. Until the body has been

IDed, or someone calls in a missing persons report, we can't take this any further."

He shook his head, looking as annoyed by the dead ends as she was. "We can't do more, Grace. I'm the first one to say keep working. But until Lewes Inc. opens, there's nothing left for us to do. The golden hour, such as it was, has already passed us by."

As they made their way back to the car, Grace felt a sense of defeat. The killer was getting bolder, crossing state lines and now targeting a woman. And they didn't have a clue who he was.

"We need some food," Dylan acknowledged. "And some rest. That way, as soon as we do have an angle to investigate, we'll be ready and prepared."

Grace nodded, feeling exhaustion start to set in. She hadn't realized how hungry she was until Dylan mentioned food.

They climbed into the car.

"I know this area, and there's a good hotel a few miles south of here," Dylan said. "Let's go there. It's close to the river and not far from the places this killer has targeted so far, and it's also close to Lewes Inc., so we can go there first thing tomorrow."

Accepting temporary defeat, for tonight at least, Grace tried to clear her mind as they drove away from the crime scene, promising herself that tomorrow would bring the results they needed.

*

An hour later, after a stop at a local diner for a burger and coffee, Grace and Dylan arrived at the hotel. On the way, Grace had called both the Arkansas and Tennessee police departments again, checking for any missing persons reports. But so far, luck wasn't on their side.

Arriving at the hotel, Grace was surprised to see that the parking lot was almost full. Walking in and looking at the signage, she found that there was an agricultural convention taking place.

"Two rooms, please?" she asked the receptionist, who looked apologetic.

"We have only one double room available," she said. "Will that suit you? It has separate beds."

Grace exchanged a glance with Dylan, feeling suddenly awkward. She hadn't expected to have to share a room.

"I - I don't mind?" she muttered.

Dylan spoke up, "That's fine. We'll take it." He handed over his ID and credit card to the receptionist and took the room key.

Then they headed upstairs to the second floor where their room was located.

Luckily, it was a spacious room, with two enormous beds a few yards apart, and a massive bathroom. Having all that space meant it was a little less awkward than she'd anticipated. But even so, there was an enforced closeness between them as they both used the bathroom in turn, making sure to give the other as much privacy as possible, showering and undressing and climbing quickly into their respective beds.

Perhaps it was that closeness that made Grace decide to take the step that was always difficult for her: getting more personal and friendly with her new partner.

"Do you want to talk about what's been happening back home, Dylan?" she asked cautiously, hoping she wasn't going to offend him with the question. "You mentioned that this new role was the best thing that had happened in a bad couple of weeks. I was wondering why?"

She wondered, as she spoke, if he might refuse to reply at all, and then she would have gotten it wrong and misjudged the dynamic completely.

She was always confident in a work situation, and when interviewing a witness or a suspect. But in a personal situation, Grace realized she was less so, and the recent friction with Tyler hadn't improved her confidence.

She waited, feeling surprisingly nervous, to see if her new partner was ready to share.

CHAPTER SIXTEEN

There was a long silence, and Grace felt her stomach twist as she realized she'd gotten it wrong, been too intrusive, and now he must be backtracking.

Just when she thought that Dylan wasn't going to reply to her question at all, he sighed, shifting in his bed so that the springs creaked softly.

"It's been a hellish time for me," he admitted. "I've been going through a divorce, after five years of marriage."

The words prompted instant sympathy in Grace, but they also scared her, as she thought about the possible breakup that might be looming in her own future.

"I'm so sorry," she said. "That must be very tough for you."

Dylan nodded, his face shadowed in the dim light of the room.

"Things just got worse and worse. It's scary how fast it can happen. One minute you're newly married and full of dreams and hope, and the next minute, you realize they've slowly eroded away and you have nothing."

"That is very scary to hear, and I guess it's impossible to stop when you're living it day by day," she said.

"I tried," he admitted. "I wanted to fix things, so badly. To get us back to where we'd been, once I realized how far we'd gone. I was going to suggest we have a whole fresh start, go for couples counseling, second honeymoon, whatever it took. But on the same night I came home with that in mind, she said she wanted a divorce. That there was no more future for us, and that she'd been seeing someone else."

Grace caught her breath at the cruel twist of fate that the timing had provided.

"Then what happened?" she asked.

"I lost it," Dylan said. "I was so mad at her for cheating. Cheating? When we were both in a permanent relationship? It was something I had never, ever expected, and it was - well, deeply shocking, I guess. But then, when I'd shouted and yelled some, I went back to blaming myself and thinking I should have done things differently, and sooner."

Grace heard the pain and anger in Dylan's voice.

"I understand why you feel that way," she said softly. "But sometimes, people just drift apart. It doesn't always have to be someone's fault."

"I know that, Grace. But it's hard not to feel like a failure. Like you're not good enough for the person you love. Now I'm sitting in a little bachelor pad. It's a temporary place, with a view of the river which is about the only thing going for it, and I'm wondering - how did it all come to this so fast? Where did the hopes and dreams go, and will I ever get them back again with someone else, or is this the end?"

"No way is it the end!" she said, now letting her fighting spirit flare. "It's a new start. You're the one who gave it a try when it was at its worst, and who acknowledged the issues. That's the sign of true character, in my book."

"You think so?" Now she heard a thread of hope in his voice, and knew her words had brought some comfort.

"I do. And I know it must feel like an insurmountable obstacle, having to deal with all of this, but at least you dealt with it. You were the one who gave it your all."

Dylan made a small noise of agreement.

"I guess losing my sister, when I was a teenager, made me feel like loss of any kind is a very big thing," he said. "You've given me a lot of comfort."

Grace pricked up her ears at the mention of his sister. That was a tragedy in his life she'd never known about, or even suspected. He'd also lost someone close to him, just as she had? But she also sensed that Dylan had spoken enough, and that he'd shared as much as he felt comfortable with.

"I am here for you," she insisted. "I might only be your work partner, but anything you need to talk about, you can. I'm not the most experienced in relationships, but I can offer all the support you want. And advice, unqualified as it might be."

Now, he gave the ghost of a laugh. "I appreciate that offer. More than you know," he admitted. "And thank you for listening."

"Any time," she said.

Turning over in bed, Grace felt deeply empathetic toward Dylan, the more so because it was awakening all her fears, and raising a whole lot of questions about the concept of permanence.

What if Tyler had proposed to her, she was now wondering. What if she had said yes, and was committed to a future with him, but he still behaved in exactly the same way as he was doing now?

The thought made her feel sick to her stomach. She had always been so sure of Tyler, so convinced that they were meant to be together. Now, as she lay in bed next to Dylan, listening to how bad a marriage could turn out, she wondered if she was just fooling herself. Was she holding onto something that wasn't meant to be?

Dylan's breathing evened out as he drifted off to sleep, and Grace lay there, staring at the ceiling, lost in thought. She knew she needed to talk to Tyler, to have an honest conversation about their future, and perhaps to insist that they go their separate ways. But the thought of it was terrifying. The upheaval. The heartache.

It was easy to understand why people ended up staying in a dysfunctional relationship, Grace realized, with a new insight into the complexities of it all.

She was sure that with all this on her mind, sleep would not come easy. But she drifted off surprisingly fast, and although she'd set her alarm for early, she was awoken by something else entirely.

*

"I'm coming for you." The words were whispered in a soft, sibilant tone, full of menace. The Southern accent resonated in them, and Grace realized in horror that she was watching her mother, in the next bed.

It wasn't Dylan any longer. It was her mother lying there, asleep in bed, on her family trip 'down South' to see the cousins that she'd taken every year. Only this year, a killer had been waiting and had gotten into the room in the cottage where her mother had stayed, and had killed her.

Time had scrolled back. She wasn't in the hotel any longer. She was in that small, thatched farmhouse cottage, watching as he was standing over her mother, a knife in his hand.

Grace's heart was pounding hard as she struggled to make sense of the situation. Was this just a nightmare, or was it really happening? Sweat beaded her forehead, and her body was trembling with fear. She had to warn her mother. Immediately. Because if she didn't wake up she would be stabbed, and fifteen year old Grace would be left without a mother in her life at all.

In that moment, Grace knew she had to do something, anything, to stop him. But what could she do? She was helpless, powerless, and utterly terrified.

The killer raised his knife, and Grace drew in a breath, ready to scream out a warning, to yell at her mother that she was in terrible danger but that, if she moved in time, she might avoid the knife wound that would otherwise pierce her heart. She might end up being okay.

But her voice wouldn't sound. It came out as a thin, trembling whisper, despite her attempts to yell as loud as she could.

It wasn't enough; she couldn't do it. She couldn't save her mother or warn her, and now, that knife was coming down, scything into her chest with a shrill screaming noise.

Just before it hit, Grace jerked awake, breathing rapidly, her heart accelerating.

There was a faint light in the window. It was morning. Dylan was in the other bed, also sitting up, groggy with sleep but quickly awakening.

And the screaming noise wasn't the knife. Nor was it her alarm.

It was someone calling, and she quickly grabbed it up.

Detective Stoll was on the line. He sounded tired and stressed, as if he'd also been jerked out of sleep by some important news.

"Agent Ford? I've just had a call. We have an ID on the body," he told her.

CHAPTER SEVENTEEN

An ID on the body? This was more than Grace had hoped for, and faster, too, since it was only five-thirty a.m.

"Who is she?" she asked Detective Stoll. Thoughts of Lewes Inc. were uppermost in her mind. As soon as she had a name, she could check on the databases and get information that might draw her theory together.

"Her name is Camille Patrick," he said. "She's a dairy farm owner in Tennessee."

"What?" Grace could hear the shock in her voice as she switched her phone to speaker, placing it on the bed so that Dylan, sitting up in the other bed, could hear this latest bombshell.

Their theory had been blown all the way apart.

Camille Patrick was not employed by Lewes Inc. She was completely different from the other two victims so far.

"A dairy farm owner?" she asked again. "Since when?"

"I believe she owns a family farm in the Tennessee area, that she inherited a couple of decades ago. One of the farm workers arrived at five a.m., and when she wasn't there to do the milking with him, he called her phone, saw that her car was still there but she wasn't picking up, and called her son, who also lives on the farm. He then arrived, opened up the house, and they called us when they realized she was nowhere to be found inside."

Grace shook her head, feeling utterly flummoxed.

"I guess we go and speak to the son," she said.

"Yes, if you could take a drive there, that'll be great. It's unfortunately right outside my jurisdiction," he said apologetically. "The other side of the river."

Grace hung up, and got moving. Quickly - with less awkwardness than there had been the night before - she and Dylan got dressed, and rushed down to the car.

It had been raining in the night, and they splashed through puddles on the damp, cold sidewalk before getting inside.

"I don't understand this," Dylan said, echoing her own thoughts. "I was so sure this had to be the company, being targeted."

"I also thought so. But now, we need to look for other common factors," Grace acknowledged.

Dylan started up, got the heater going, and then they headed out in the direction of the nearest river bridge to lead them over the Mississippi and to Camille Patrick's dairy farm.

It occurred to her, as they rode over the bridge spanning the gray, flowing water in the murky morning light, that the only common factor so far was the river itself.

*

When Grace and Dylan arrived at the farm, which bordered the Mississippi a few miles to the north, she saw immediately that the people in this area had rallied. Three pickups and two sedans were parked outside the wooden farmhouse. Two workers were herding cattle out of the barn and into a nearby pasture. The home's front door stood open.

"I think I'll go and speak to the workers," Dylan suggested. "They might know something."

"Good idea." Grace was happy with this time saving tactic. "I'll go inside and speak to the son."

Grace headed straight inside, in search of Camille Patrick's son. She headed to the living room, hearing voices coming from there.

A shocked-looking man, tall and burly, with the same pale blonde hair as she remembered seeing on the victim, was standing in the middle of the room, surrounded by a small knot of other people. Everyone looked dressed for the outdoor working day, in waterproof jackets, jeans, and boots. Five tanned and weathered faces turned her way.

"Excuse me for the interruption," Grace said, "I'm FBI Agent Ford. I'm here to investigate the murder of Camille Patrick. I'm so very sorry for your loss," she said to the young man, and also included everyone in the room, knowing that in such a community the correct pleasantries had to be observed. Then, turning to the young man, she asked, "Are you her son?"

The tall man nodded, his face drawn and uncomprehending. "I'm Barry Patrick," he agreed.

The room had obviously been furnished by his mother. Floral couches, an antique clock, and deep pink curtains all pointed to a feminine touch. There were photos on the mantelpiece of prize cows with blue ribbons around their necks, and a few amateur-looking watercolor landscapes were mounted on the walls.

Grace took a deep breath, trying to appear sympathetic but professional at the same time. "I'm here to ask you a few questions about your mother, Mr. Patrick, if that's alright with you."

With a shuffling of feet, and mutterings about needing privacy, the others in the room made way, some heading outside, and a couple retreating to the adjacent kitchen, leaving her alone with Barry.

"Sure," Barry said, his voice shaky. "But I don't understand why anyone would want to hurt her. I doubt I can tell you much. She was just a hard-working dairy farmer, minding her own business."

Grace took a moment to size him up. He was a big guy, likely weighing over two hundred pounds and standing over six feet tall. He had a rugged face with a strong jaw line and bright blue eyes. His skin was tanned and lined from years of working outside, and his hands were rough and calloused. But the expression in his face was like a lost little boy, and she felt deeply sorry for him.

"Did your mother have any enemies? Anyone who might have wanted to harm her, or any issues in her life that were problematic?" Grace asked.

Barry shook his head. "No, not that I know of. I mean, she was trying to get the farm back on track. She managed it with a partner who'd allowed it to get out of hand while she focused on the dairy product manufacture side. Artisanal cheeses, that sort of thing. It was going well, but back at the farm, things were less so. The manure wasn't being properly disposed of and the place was in a mess. She recently got rid of the partner and started afresh, got it in shape again, but this wasn't his doing, I'm sure of it."

"Why's that?" Grace asked.

"Because he was from Canada and he went back up there when the partnership dissolved a few months ago. He moved back to join his nephew in a lumber business there, and it's apparently doing well."

Grace nodded. "Okay, that's good information. Can you think of anyone else who might have a motive for harming your mother? Maybe a disgruntled employee, or a neighbor who didn't like her?"

He shook his head. "I helped out with the staff payments, the hiring contracts, that sort of thing. Everyone was happy. And the neighbors are all here now. They're like, lifelong friends," he said with a sad shrug.

"Did your mother have any connection with a firm called Lewes Inc.?" she asked. "Did she know Thomas Lane or Jim Penney?"

He shook his head. "Thomas Lane? I think I remember that name? He's the first guy who was murdered, right? People were talking about it, over the past few days, since he was found just across the river. But I don't know either of those guys, and I'm sure Mom also didn't. I don't recall her mentioning the names."

"And where were you last night?" she asked, since Detective Stoll had said he lived on site.

"I was transporting cattle out of state," he explained. "I got back in the small hours of the morning, and went straight to sleep in my cottage, which is up on the hill there, on the other side of the main barn. I was woken up by Sam, the early morning worker, banging on my door."

Grace thanked him, and after offering a few more words of comfort, she turned and left.

Her heart plummeted as she walked out of the small farmhouse. They were no further along. Her questioning had only resulted in more dead ends.

But as she looked toward the cattle shed, she saw Dylan hurrying out, and the expression in his face told her immediately that he'd gotten something. There was excitement in his eyes and purpose in every line of his body as he waved at her.

She rushed over to find out if this was the breakthrough that they needed.

CHAPTER EIGHTEEN

"Grace," Dylan said, his voice so taut that her spine prickled. "We've got a brand new lead."

"What is it?" she asked. This was the lifeline they needed, and one that would hopefully reset the course of this case. At the moment it was veering into disaster.

"I just got called by the detective in charge on the Tennessee side," he said. "And he just got called himself by police in Missouri. A criminal escaped custody a week ago in St. Louis. They think he might have fled south, crossed state lines, and may be committing these murders now. They've pulled together a few eyewitness reports and crime incidents that confirm the direction he's fled."

“Who is this criminal?” she asked, as they both headed purposefully to the car.

"His name's Billy Wilson," he said.

"And his history? What's his criminal background?"

"He was arrested after beating up a colleague, gagging him with a sock, and attempting to drown him. And that follows a string of other violent offenses."

Now, her pulse was quickening. This sounded like a seriously strong lead.

"Do they have any other details? Where are they hunting for him?"

"Details are coming through as we speak. I'll give you my iPad and you can check them out. We're going to drive north, and communicate with the other teams on the way. They're pinpointing a few likely areas. I said that we'll take whichever one we're closest to."

Grace got in the car, opened the iPad, and, as they drove north, she read out the details that the team was messaging through.

"Billy Wilson escaped from a holding cell a week ago, while awaiting trial. If you follow the three places where he was sighted, or where violent incidents occurred, they're all heading south of St. Louis. He was fleeing this way, for sure. They even identified him on camera footage at a convenience store he robbed. Here's a picture of him."

Dylan glanced at the iPad before veering onto the highway, looking at the picture of Billy's face. Then, Grace stared down at it, taking in this man’s broad forehead, his mouth, with a twisted scar on his cheek, and his dark, heavy brows. She needed to imprint this face in her mind so that she would know, at a glance, if they found him.

"The police are cooperating across the state lines, and the manhunt has been extended into Arkansas. It’s getting under way as we speak. Okay, so this is where they think he’s likely to be. Messages are coming through fast.” Now, Grace scrolled past the face picture and kept reading aloud, updating Dylan further.

"They're noting the fact he has family in southern Arkansas, and also that the forest is a known hideout for drifters and criminals."

She identified the coordinates.

"Take the next turnoff," she advised Dylan.

This was sounding promising. Given the fact that Camille Patrick’s farm was so close to this hideout, and that the other two men had been dumped in nearby areas along the river, there was a strong chance it could be his work.

"Are there any reports of stolen cars?" she wondered out loud, thinking that the victims would have had to be transported to their final watery dumping grounds.

Dylan raised his eyebrows, glancing at the iPad. “You should be able to access the case info from there. Just go through the menu on the left. The password should come up automatically.”

She navigated the menu, logged in, and quickly checked the databases.

Yes, was the answer. There were a few reports of stolen vehicles in the area, ranging from a few hours to a couple of days after Billy Wilson's escape.

"So, could he have transported them?" Dylan asked.

"Yes," she said. There was only one stolen vehicle - a motorcycle - that wouldn't have been able to do that job.

As Dylan sped along the main road, with Grace directing him as the messages from the team came through on the radio, Grace dialed the number for the detective in charge of the manhunt, and was soon communicating with him.

The officer, speaking in a strong Southern accent, sounded sharp, professional, motivated, and a world away from the lackadaisical attitude of the weary Detective Stoll.

"We've got a few different locations that are being searched," he said sharply. "The forest bordering the river is one of the two most likely locations, and we've put a team of six men in there, as well as two patrol cars around the perimeter. I'm leading the team, and we're currently on the way through from a trail head in the north of the forest. Give me your coordinates and I'll tell you where the best starting point will be."

Grace checked the iPad and read them out, and after a pause, the officer replied.

"I'm going to direct you to the most southerly part of the woods. That way you'll come up and meet us, and he'll be cut off if he tries to escape that way."

"Sounds good," Grace said. Already, she was running through the necessary protocols in her mind. It had been a long time since she'd done a forest pursuit. Recently, all her manhunts and takedowns had been in an urban setting. She thought back to her training, refreshing herself on what she would need to have top of mind for this mission.

Alertness, perceptiveness, peripheral vision, and agility. Moving quietly and keeping aware of the surroundings would be crucial. As Dylan sped onto the dirt road leading to the trail head, Grace aligned the priorities in her head.

The terse communications on the radio told her that everyone was moving into place. Grace checked her iPad again.

“I think it should be here,” she said, staring ahead at where the coordinates were leading them. The forest was thick and dark, and the road leading up to the trailhead was poorly maintained, full of potholes. The car bounced over them.

“You sure this is the right way?” Dylan asked.

“I think it is,” Grace replied. She felt thoroughly disoriented, but the coordinates were definitely pointing ahead. “I’ve messaged him to check. I don’t want to interrupt the radio conversation by asking for directions. He’s texting back now.” She glanced down again. “Yes, he says it is very isolated and hardly ever used. We must look for the trail head leading into the woods. There it is! And now he’s going to pinpoint a couple of the most likely areas within the woods where he could be. Abandoned cabins, and the like.”

They reached a break in the trees, and found the trail head, which seemed to be seldom used. The wooden sign had fallen over on its side, and the grass was long and straggly.

“Look at it this way. If you’re an escaped convict who knows these woods, this is going to be a great hiding place,” she pointed out.

“I guess you’re right. So let’s go hunting,” Dylan agreed. He sent in a message on the radio. “We’re in place now, and setting off.”

Then he took the radio out of the car and fastened it onto his belt.

Climbing out of the car, Grace checked her weapon, pulled on her jacket, and set off into the woods, with Dylan walking alongside.

In a minute, they were in a completely different world.

The forest was thick and quiet, with only the occasional sound of twigs snapping underfoot, and the faint chirping of birds overhead. Grace felt her senses sharpen as they headed deeper. The air was damp, cooler than outside, and the terrain varied from muddy soil to stony stretches as the trail traversed the hillside.

When the path narrowed, Dylan took the lead, searching for the first pin drop, and Grace followed closely behind, staying alert for any sounds out of the ordinary.

With the trees hemming them in, Grace was very aware of how exposed they were as they walked, and that unfriendly eyes might be watching from a multitude of hiding places as they passed.

If someone was watching them, would they see that person in turn?

"This is the first place," Dylan whispered. She felt impressed by his navigational skill, as he headed unerringly to the left. They followed an almost invisible trail that wound its way up through the trees, ending at a disused cabin. Looming up in the woods ahead, the tumbledown structure looked like something out of a nightmare, or a dark fairytale. The wood was deeply stained and scarred, and an entire section seemed to have been scorched by a fire in the past.

She could see the door ahead, warped and misaligned with the doorway. They stopped, watched, listened.

Nothing to be heard. Now, the silence rang in their ears.

"Shall we try the door?" Grace whispered.

She strode forward, trying to keep her footfalls soundless as she reached it, prepared herself, turned on her flashlight, and then shoved it sharply open.

She heard a scuttling inside and tensed immediately, her hand moving to her gun. But the sound was too faint. It wasn't a human. And her flashlight beam, when she trained it in that direction, found nothing.

The cabin was empty, and looked to have been that way for some time. Inside was deserted, apart from some broken wooden planks and a pile of moldy rags. No trace of recent human occupation. Wherever Billy was, he wasn't here.

"We press on?" Grace asked.

“Yes. This track should take us where we need to go.” He glanced at the map, and the directions, again. Leaving the cabin, Dylan took a different route out, heading on a diagonal path.

"The next hiding place is at the foot of that mountain," he said. "And according to these instructions, it's a natural cave. I guess a cave would be my first choice if I knew this area and came here. This is where he'd go, I think."

Grace trusted Dylan’s instincts, especially since he seemed so at home in the woods. And, treading behind him, as they neared the foot of the mountain and the trail got thicker and more overgrown, she picked up a distinctive smell.

Wood smoke.

Someone had lit a fire, not long ago, in the gaping mouth of the cave that loomed ahead.

Were they still inside?

Knowing that they could be face-to-face with the killer at any moment, she crept forward to find out.

CHAPTER NINETEEN

Grace turned her flashlight on again, shining it into the cave's dark mouth. The beam reflected off the haze of smoke, almost blinding her, so that she moved it away.

Was anyone in here? Now Dylan's flashlight was also blasting through the smoke, piercing into the cave's mouth.

No. The cave was empty. Now that they had moved past the smoldering ashes, the light was reflecting off the rocky back wall.

But there were signs someone had been here, apart from the fire itself. There were a couple of food wrappers, and a few discarded bones, and a folded item right at the back that looked like a rough blanket. Someone had cooked and eaten here, and perhaps they'd slept here, also.

"Looks to me like someone camped out here for the night," Dylan whispered.

Grace nodded in agreement. It seemed like a logical place for someone to hide out in. But now the question was, where had the killer gone?

"He might have moved on, but might also have gone out to hunt, or get water," Dylan said. He was whispering, but even so, it felt as if the closeness of the forest was swallowing his voice.

,"I see two trails leading out of here, apart from the one we were on," Grace said, walking out of the empty cave to examine the surrounding terrain.

"Yes. One leads down to the river, and one leads up the slope and around the mountain," he said, consulting the map.

Grace thought about what the movements of a fugitive might be. "The river might be the best option?" she suggested.

Dylan shrugged. "If he's gone to hunt then yes. But if he's moving on, the path around the mountaintop is a wider and more direct route, so he could get somewhere else faster."

Grace frowned. "If they're both strong possibilities, then it makes sense for us to split up here?"

"I don't like the thought of that," Dylan countered. "We're chasing a man who might have killed three times. Splitting up is not a sensible idea. And we have only one radio."

Grace quirked a challenging eyebrow. "Give me a better idea, then," she said. "Both these routes sound viable, and he's left recently. If we pick the wrong one, we might lose him."

Eventually, Dylan capitulated.

“Okay, then. You take the path around the mountaintop and I'll head down to the river. But we need to be extra careful, and if we see or hear anything, we need to make sure we alert each other straight away, and also let the search party know."

“Of course,” Grace agreed.

He activated his radio, which he'd had on silent for the approach to the cave. Immediately the crackle of communication filtered in. The team was searching hard, but after only a few seconds of listening, Grace realized they hadn't found the fugitive.

Dylan updated the team.

"He's not in the cabin or the cave. We're splitting up now to search the area, and each taking a different track."

Then he snapped the radio off again. They only had one between them, and that meant Grace would have only her phone for communication.

"We stay in touch," she said.

Grace watched Dylan take off towards the river, soon out of sight, disappearing into the dense foliage. She turned and began to follow the path that wound its way around the mountain. Though clearly marked, the trail was steep and treacherous, and she had to be careful not to slip on the loose rocks. It was a challenge to keep her footing, while also looking out for any signs of this criminal.

What was that ahead?

She froze, all her instincts flaring, as she saw a shape ahead, just past a bend in the path, beyond a tall tree.

Was it him? The form was standing still, in the dark shade of the tree, and as she walked quietly toward it, Grace put her hand on the grip of her gun. She was not taking any chances. She was not going to assume this person was innocent. So far they were staying very still, and that in itself was suspicious. Had they seen her?

Get closer first, she urged herself. Get closer before you alert him.

But as she neared the shape, the form slowly changed. The arms, that she'd thought were twisted with muscle, became knotted branches.

The head became a thick cluster of leaves. The body was nothing more than a tree trunk, in the shadow of its partner.

Just a tree.

Grace breathed a sigh of relief. She was on edge and knew she needed to steady herself. The adrenaline pumping through her body was making her jumpy, and she was seeing things that weren't there.

She looked carefully around her, left and right, peering into the woods, making sure. She was about to continue, when from behind her, far back down the trail, she heard a shout.

Grace froze, her heart now pumping fast.

Had that been Dylan? Or just her senses playing tricks on her again?

She turned, indecision flooding through her straining her ears for any sound that could confirm if what she'd heard was right, or just an illusion.

For a moment there was nothing. But then, she heard another shout, and this time she was certain she recognized Dylan's voice.

Grace sprinted back the way she had come, her body taut with urgency, her feet skidding on the stones which were even more treacherous on the way down.

Dylan was in trouble. He must be. That shout had told her so.

She didn't know what was happening, but she knew Dylan had a crisis on the go. She sprinted down the winding path, her feet pounding against the rocks and dirt. The shouts grew louder, and she could now hear a commotion, the sound of something being smashed.

She reached the cave and powered past it, heading along the steep downhill, sliding on the stones and regaining her balance, allowing her naturally fast reactions to kick in and save her, with the smell and sound of the rushing river now in her ears.

And ahead of her, she saw a shocking sight.

On the edge of a steep drop in the path, about forty yards away, Dylan was struggling frantically with a tall, heavyset man.

There was no way she could use her gun here. Dylan was closer to her, and if she shot at the man, she risked hitting him.

As she got closer, she could see that the man was bigger than Dylan, and he had a crazed look in his eyes as he fought. He wasn't looking to attack. He was looking to flee.

Grace rushed forward to join in the fray. Piecing together what must have happened, she guessed that Dylan had surprised the man in hiding and had managed to get close enough to grab him. But he was struggling furiously to get away, with a heavier weight and all the strength of desperation on his side.

Was this the convict they were hunting? She glimpsed his features and she thought they matched well enough with the ones etched in her mind.

They needed to take him down, before he broke away and fled. But as she raced up to the scene, their fugitive landed a well-placed kick, his boot lashing into Dylan's knee.

Dylan's leg buckled and he staggered back, dropping down with a cry of pain. The heavyset man turned and began to race away.

Now, the clock was ticking. Grace had to catch up, or he'd disappear into those woods.

CHAPTER TWENTY

Dylan was scrambling to his feet, staggering, clutching a tree for support, and worry for him filled Grace as she sprinted toward him. "Are you okay? Is it bad?" she shouted.

"I'll be fine. Go get him!" he shouted, gesturing ahead with his free hand. "I'll radio the others!"

No time for more. There was a criminal to catch. Grace hated to leave her partner, it went against all her instincts, but there was no choice, not now. She raced along the track in the direction he'd fled, doing her utmost to gain ground, knowing it all rested on her shoulders.

But that attack had worked in his favor, and given him a sizeable lead. The man who they suspected was Billy Wilson, was running hard, and Grace knew that if he got too far ahead of her, he might disappear into the vast expanse of trees and undergrowth. He must know these woods well. He certainly seemed to have found the bolt hole he needed. And they were unfamiliar territory to her.

He was fast, but from the pounding of his footfalls and the shape of him, she saw that he wasn't only a bulky man, but a heavy runner. Some big men were light on their feet. Not him. She was slender in build, and light when she ran, and Grace knew that although she wasn't lethally fast, her endurance was her strong point. In the FBI training exercises, the men had always outpaced her - at the start. And then, as the miles and the obstacles had progressed, she'd caught them up. One by one, inexorably, running past the flagging men, leaving them behind as she maintained her speed on legs that were slim but steely.

Grace knew she'd need to draw on this same endurance now. It was the only weapon she had. She couldn't get a clear shot at the man, and in any case, there was not sufficient cause for her to shoot a fleeing man in the back. This had to be done the hard way.

She ran on, getting into a rhythm, letting her legs take her forward, keeping her breathing regular. And now, she saw that her endurance was getting results, because ahead, her suspect was starting to flag.

He suddenly veered to the left, hoping to throw her off his trail. But Grace was listening as well as watching, and she heard the crash of his footsteps in the undergrowth. She followed him, spying an almost hidden trail, sprinting deeper into the forest with branches snagging at her jacket and catching at her feet on this narrower track. But he was bigger, more solid, and there was more of him to be slowed down.

This detour hadn't helped him, and now she was gaining, drawing closer until the gap could be measured by a few yards, and then by a few feet.

Grace decided she was close enough, now, to try a tackle. Bracing herself, she surged forward, leaping at him, using her momentum to unbalance him, grabbing onto him as tight as she could.

As he crashed to the ground, her elbow broke her own fall and landed squarely on his solar plexus. The breath whooshed out of him.

As quickly as she could, she pressed home her advantage, getting one of the handcuffs around his wrists. Now for the other. That was harder; her gasping fugitive was getting his breath back.

With a gasp of rage, fists flailing, he began to struggle.

She ducked under his flying arm, made another grab for it, and got it. Now to hold on, but he was twisting away, using all his weight against her. She couldn't let him go, and she had to get that second cuff fastened.

"You're not getting away!" she threatened him, hanging on grimly. "This is it!"

"You can't get me on your own!" he retorted, aiming a kick that would have disabled her knee even worse than Dylan's if she hadn't writhed out of the way in time. She almost let go, but managed to keep her grip.

She could use a third hand now, Grace thought, as the big man began to aim furious kicks at her again, sending mud and leaves showering around her. But a moment later she got something even better.

A whole new pair of hands.

Footsteps thudded behind her and relief flooded her as Dylan closed in, at a limping jog. He flung himself into the fray, grabbing their captive's other arm and forcing it behind him, staggering as he tried to stand squarely on his uninjured leg. But that intervention was enough. Over Billy's cries of "No! No! This is police brutality!" the second cuff clicked closed.

As she and Dylan dragged the man to his feet, Grace got her first clear sight of him.

At close quarters, she clearly recognized that broad forehead, those heavy brows.

This was the escaped convict. Thanks to Dylan's knowledge of the terrain and her speed, they'd captured him.

Now to find out if he was the killer.

*

Half an hour later, Billy Wilson was sitting opposite Grace and Dylan in the small interview room of the local Tennessee police station. His broad face was flushed. His cheeks were darkened with a few days' worth of stubble. His thick brows were scowling.

While they were interrogating him, Grace knew the other members of the search party would have arrived at the cave where he'd spent some time and lit that fire. They would be looking for any evidence to link him to the crimes.

But Billy himself had become his own biggest defender.

"Look, the charges I was arrested for were false," he pleaded, in a surprisingly high-pitched voice. "They were all trumped up. All I was doing was claiming my right to freedom!"

He stared from Grace to Dylan and back again.

Grace shook her head. "You were convicted of serious crimes, Mr. Wilson. You can't go on the run to prove your innocence. Doing that works the opposite way. But that aside, what I want to know now is where you've been the past few days. And what you've been doing."

He was silent, pressing his lips together. This wasn't going to be easy. They weren't going to get answers from him readily. But they needed them.

"I'm not going to downplay the situation. You're in trouble," Grace said. "But that trouble is only going to get worse if you don't answer us. Additional charges will end up on that sheet. Right now, if you cooperate, you've got more of a chance of making your life easier."

She paused, letting the words sink in. "You've been in jail before; you know what it's like there. You know you can be treated better, or you can get the worst treatment. You can be sent to the prison with the worst reputation, and get the nastiest cell, with no hope of early parole. If you want your life to be better, and maybe for us to put in a good word for you, you need to do your part. Now."

He shifted, easing his handcuffed wrists which rested on the table. Then, he took a deep breath and she saw that he'd made a decision.

He was ready to talk.

"I don't know what to say," he said. "All I've been doing is keeping away from people. Why are you so interested in where I've been?"

"Where have you been?" Dylan pressured.

He shrugged. "Living in the cave! It wasn't great; it was cold, but I wanted the heat to die down, you know?"

"So you've been spending how long there?"

"Three days, I think," he admitted. "Why do you keep asking? Has something else happened that you're trying to pin on me?" A crafty note now crept into his voice.

Dylan glanced at Grace.

Grace leaned forward. "What were you doing in the cave for three days, Billy?"

He hesitated. "Sheltering. I had to keep in hiding, keep away from anyone who might turn me in. I was just trying to survive."

"You stole a car to get there, didn't you?" she asked.

"Stole a car! I never did such a thing!" He sounded appalled.

"Borrowed one, then?"

"I didn't steal nor borrow no car," he insisted. "I don't even know how to drive! I never took that test. I didn't want to get far. I hitchhiked with a truck driver, and then walked the last few miles. That's how I got there. I know this part of the world, slightly."

"And the river? Did you go down there?"

He shook his head adamantly.

"That river is poisoned. Why would I go there? Everyone knows you don't touch that water. I used clean water, from the forest streams."

"And did you see anyone while you were in that forest?"

He shook his head. "How many times must I tell you? I was avoiding folk!"

Grace's phone buzzed and she looked quickly down to check it. It was a message from the two officers who'd been searching the cave.

"Bread, berries, a sharpened stick, and an old blanket. No sign of any abandoned vehicles in the area."

Quickly, Grace got up and walked out. She called the officer as soon as the interview room door had closed.

"Thanks so much for the update. Are you sure about the vehicle?" she asked.

"Yes. We knew how important it was to find one nearby, so we had our patrol vehicles search all the roads, and we even sent a drone up to check. There were two vehicles parked in the area, both in the possession of their rightful owners, who were fishing and hiking. We called them to check."

Grace thanked him again, and hung up. Then, she frowned. This was not adding up.

She was beginning to accept, reluctantly, that they had caught a criminal, but not the criminal they needed. This man had been avoiding people, but he hadn't had cotton wool on him for the gag, or rope for the ties, and there was no sign of a car in the wider area. He would have needed to use a car, and recently, too, to access and transport all the victims. Especially since they lived miles apart from each other, and two of them lived miles from the river.

Logistically he could not have done it.

She opened the interview room door again, and called Dylan out.

Once they were both standing outside, she showed him the message and told him about the car. "With no vehicle, he's not our man," she said.

"I'm also having difficulty with the logistics. They don't add up," Dylan admitted. He was still limping, even though he'd insisted his knee was fine. She could see it was hurting. A lot. He'd gotten injured in a violent takedown and they had nothing to show for it.

"I reckon we hand him over to the local police, and we keep looking."

Dylan nodded grimly. "I guess we have to. But where? That's the question."

Grace folded her arms and thought back over the case so far.

There were a lot of things that were bothering her. A lot of unanswered questions, and many things she thought people were hiding. But she didn't know if any of them were relevant. People kept secrets for all sorts of reasons. What would get them further in the case? What did these victims have in common, why had they been chosen, why had they been killed in the way they had? Where was the thread that they were missing?

As she was thinking furiously about this, her phone started buzzing again. This time, it was a local number that she didn't recognize.

She picked up the call, and found herself speaking to Dr. Rodriguez, who'd handled the first two postmortems.

“Agent Ford?” she asked.

“Speaking,” Grace said.

“Remember, I said I’d send off that gag for tox screening?” Rodriguez asked. “It came back, faster than I expected. And I’ve got a surprising result.”

CHAPTER TWENTY ONE

"A result?" Grace switched the phone onto speaker so that Dylan could also hear. Standing there, in the corridor outside the interview room, they listened to what the doctor had to say about those strange, cotton-padded gags.

"Yes," the doc replied. "That gag was soaked in a toxic mix of chemicals. We picked up mercury, formalin, benzene, and a trace of organic phosphorus."

"What?" Grace said, her voice incredulous. This was an astonishing development. This didn't seem like accidental contamination, or even something specific like chloroform, which she'd been thinking might be picked up. This was a carefully chosen mix of poisons. Deliberately done, for sure.

Dylan's eyes widened in shock. "That's lethal. Most likely, they were unable to struggle by the time they went into the water. But how could someone get ahold of all those chemicals? Any idea on that, Doc?"

"They're all commercially available in various forms," Rodriguez explained. "Even liquid mercury can be bought legally through a laboratory. But yes, in combination, that toxic mix could cause loss of consciousness, paralysis, convulsions, and ultimately, even death, if the victims hadn't drowned."

Grace nodded slowly, processing the information. The gags, as much as the river, had killed those victims. But who would have used them and more importantly, what was the message the killer was sending?

This information was going to take them in a new direction. Thanking the doctor for her speedy analysis, she hung up and turned to Dylan.

"The killer must have these chemicals stored somewhere. And a motive for using them, too."

He nodded. "The question is – where do we go from here?"

"Chemicals are pointing all the way back to Lewes Inc. again," she said.

Leaving the interview room, she headed toward the police station's lobby. Dylan walked beside her, his gaze still questioning.

"You want to go back there? Think you'll get more out of them?"

"I don't want to go back there. Not now."

"So then what?" He looked at her quizzically.

"Let's hand Billy over and let the local police question him. He's not our guy, and they can take over from here with the original charges. But I know there's one person we've spoken to so far who needs to give us better answers. There's one person who's hiding things we need to know more about. Especially in light of what we've just discovered."

She saw understanding dawn in Dylan's eyes as she continued.

"That person is Alex Stratton. I know he's keeping secrets that he refused to tell us."

"Yes, he did," Dylan agreed. "He was adamant he wasn't going to break the rules of that agreement he signed."

"We have to come on stronger. Whatever it takes, we have to make him talk."

*

Half an hour later, Grace and Dylan arrived at Stratton's large, immaculately kept house for the second time.

She knew he wasn't the killer. He had an alibi that they'd confirmed. But she was certain that he was hiding information that could get them closer. This time, they needed to come on strong, and pressurize this entitled, arrogant man into giving up what he knew.

Outside the house, a garden services van was parked, and two men in green overalls were tending the neat yard. Grace nodded a greeting to them as she walked up to the front door, hoping that Stratton would be at home, and not playing golf.

Grace knocked firmly on the door; within seconds, she heard footsteps approach and it opened. There was Alex, dressed in a Polo golf shirt, the sky blue fabric contrasting with his tanned arms and face.

She had a feeling that the presence of the garden services van had helped them, and that Alex had thought the landscapers were calling him outside. At any rate, he looked shocked to see them on his doorstep again. Shocked enough that Dylan quickly got his foot into place, to prevent him from trying to slam it in their faces again.

"What do you want now?" Alex demanded rudely, his eyes flickering back and forth between Grace and Dylan.

"We need to talk to you again," Grace said. "May we come in?"

"What is this about? You already questioned me." Annoyance resounded in his voice. "I've got a golf game organized. I need to leave in ten minutes."

That might be a good thing. The short timeframe might make him anxious to get going, and more willing to spill what he knew. Especially if he could be convinced that the FBI wouldn't leave before he told them.

"You're not going anywhere until you answer some more questions," Grace said, ignoring Alex's desire to cut the conversation short. "We've got some new information about the case and we need to know more from you now."

Alex shook his head. "I already told you what I could," he said, his tone dismissive.

"Can we speak inside?" Dylan asked. "Or do you want the landscapers to overhear our conversation?"

With an angry shrug, Alex capitulated. He turned and stalked into the immaculate living room where they'd spoken the last time.

"Your payoff," Grace said, getting immediately to the point. "How much was it?"

He narrowed his eyes. "I already said, I can't speak about that. I signed a non-disclosure agreement and I consider it binding. I respect my ex-employer's confidentiality requirements."

Grace exchanged a meaningful look with Dylan before continuing.

"Unfortunately, a criminal case overrides what you signed in a severance agreement," Grace told him. "We need to know what you signed this agreement for. What were you paid, and what were you told not to talk about? Because I don't buy that it was your insider knowledge and chemical formulations. I think there was something more to it."

She watched his face carefully and saw the subtle shift in his expression.

Grace knew she was right. This man was hiding something he'd been told not to talk about. And she knew for sure there was a lot at stake here.

Alex crossed his arms in front of him. "Even if I did know something more, why should I tell you? I have no reason to want to cooperate with you."

"Is avoiding criminal charges a good enough reason?" Grace asked. "If you don't cooperate, you will be facing serious consequences, by which I mean a criminal conviction. We are going to press charges right now and I don't think your non-disclosure agreement will protect you."

Alex's eyes widened in alarm and Grace knew she had hit a nerve. She pressed on.

"We know that you were paid off to keep quiet about something that may well be related to this case. And we know that you're hiding information that could help us solve it. So, unless you want to face the consequences, you need to start talking now."

Alex swallowed, his eyes darting between Grace and Dylan.

"That jail time is not a joke," Dylan said, his voice almost apologetic. "We're bound by the law to do what we have to, you know. In a recent case in Louisiana, I arrested a company director for exactly the same thing. He refused to give us information, and he ended up spending three days inside, and a fortune on lawyer's fees and bail money, and he now has a criminal conviction. And guess what? He ended up telling us what he knew. And he could have done it the easy way at the start, and gone off to enjoy a golf game. So can you. Otherwise, trust me, it will get nasty, and it will get expensive. And if we end up in court then your ex-employer will know about it regardless."

They waited.

The silence stretched out, laced with tension. Alex was blinking rapidly, his fists clenched in his lap.

After a full minute, he slumped back in his chair, defeated. "Fine," he said. "I'll tell you what I know."

CHAPTER TWENTY TWO

Grace kept a poker face as Alex Stratton blurted out the words. Inside, though, triumph surged, because at last, they were going to find out what they needed.

"Why did you sign that agreement with Lewes Inc.?" she asked. "And this time, we need the full reasons for it. Give us the truth."

"I could get into so much trouble for this," Alex muttered, glancing out of the large, plate glass window. But she knew he realized that trouble waited for him, no matter what he decided to do, and that if he didn't cooperate it would be worse.

"Your company can't force you to stay quiet about anything when the police come knocking," she added. Now, she saw that he was drawing some reassurance from the words. Not that he deserved it, because whatever it was, he'd been complicit in it.

But maybe, under that blustery, defensive, entitled façade, there was also a need to tell what he knew. Most people didn't like carrying a guilty secret around with them.

And although she didn't think he was a particularly good man, she did believe that most people had a shred of decency.

"You need to tell us what it was. We're not going to prosecute you for it, whatever it is. Even if what you did was illegal. Right now, finding the killer is our priority."

After taking a deep breath, he began speaking.

"Thank you for that reassurance. Look, from the get-go, it was not my fault. I just happened to be involved."

"Understood," Grace said.

"A couple of months before I was forced to leave because of the management issues, I became aware of something that Lewes Inc. kept very quiet. You see, they'd been accumulating a lot of excess toxic waste products that they couldn't dispose of easily. Well, they could have, but for logistical reasons it would have been very expensive to do that, and the directors and shareholders wanted to see a good profit in that quarter."

"What did they do with the waste?" Grace asked.

Alex hesitated, his eyes flicking between Grace and Dylan.

"They dumped it. In the river," he finally admitted.

Grace's stomach twisted with disgust and anger. But she didn't let those emotions show. Not now that Alex was finally talking.

"Over what time period?"

"It happened over a few months. Probably over the better part of a year, a couple of years ago."

"Anyone else involved with this?"

"Look, it was - it was a complicated exercise, because the river is tested regularly by state water inspectors. So they - they paid off one of the inspectors to falsify the test results." Now that he'd been forced to confess to this, he was flushing a deep red.

"And they made you sign an agreement to keep quiet about it?"

"Yes. That was why the payoff was so large. I was told to stay quiet and sign the agreement. And they threatened major legal action if I refused."

Grace could feel her blood boiling. To think that a company would prioritize profit over the health and safety of the environment and the people living around it was sickening.

"Who else was involved?"

"Well, the teams in the factory and dispatch played a role, I believe. There was a temporary pipeline set up. From what I heard, one crew was told it would be to pump water out. Another was told that the pipeline was going to a storage tank. It was done very carefully, but I ended up realizing what was going on," he said defensively.

"And so you paid off an inspector?" Dylan confirmed.

"The company did that! Not me."

"But you knew about it?"

"Yes, I was the one who had to deliver the money to the inspector. It was a lot of money, and it was all done in cash, of course," Alex muttered. "There was some excuse made for it, but it was obviously a bribe. Anyone could see that."

"Were there any consequences for the inspector?" Grace asked.

"How would I know that?" he asked.

"Because I'm thinking you do. You might have kept your eyes and ears open, seeing as how you two shared a guilty secret," Grace accused him.

Alex pressed his lips together, looking at his tightly clasped fingers.

"We'll find out anyway," Dylan said. "When you said you'd tell what you knew, the deal was to tell everything. So go on. Say it."

Alex glanced at the window again, as if wishing he was outside, and not stuck here with two police officers in an atmosphere that was becoming increasingly threatening. He was looking everywhere but at them.

"Look, I didn't know at the time. But after you came around asking me questions, I checked up on him. Just in case, because I felt I needed to know and I guess I had a lot of guilt flooding back. And I found out, this morning, actually, that he has been fired. I don't know if it was to do with that. And I didn't follow the whole story. It might have been for something else. I don't know. Like I said, I've been keeping my nose out of things after I signed that document. I haven't been asking questions or looking into anything."

Grace and Dylan exchanged a glance. This was a major breakthrough in their case. They had just uncovered a large-scale environmental crime that had been covered up by a powerful corporation.

More importantly, they had a new suspect.

A corrupt inspector who'd suffered consequences for his criminal actions. He'd been fired. And perhaps that meant someone had talked.

He might have been looking to get payback. He might even have received other bribes. Perhaps Camille Patrick's dairy farm partner had also had the opportunity to pay him off after those polluting activities escalated.

"Give me the inspector's name, please," she said.

Now, Alex was fidgeting uneasily.

"Look, please. This is going to backlash on me. Please keep my name out of this if you can," he stammered out, sounding very different from the aggressive, entitled man who'd opened the door to them. Now, he was acknowledging the extent of what he'd done, the trouble he'd been complicit in. Until now, he'd been so conveniently shielded from it, by his company and by the money going around. A big payout to him when he left, and the rest to the inspector whose name Grace was sure they were going to pry out of him.

"We do keep information confidential unless it's specifically relevant," Grace said firmly.

"I don't know if I remember," he tried.

"Give us the name," Dylan pressured.

"It's...it's Inspector Randall," Alex finally revealed, reluctance clear in his voice.

"Thank you," Dylan said, scribbling the name in his notebook. He looked up. "You mentioned you met him, to hand over the cash? Where does he live? I assume you know the area, if not the address."

"He lives near Jonesboro," Alex says. "Jonesboro is where those state offices are based. I really don't know his address, but we met at a park near his house. I've told you everything I know."

He looked appalled now, as if a wall of denial had been broken down and he'd seen the person he'd become. At least now, they had the truth.

Grace got up. Furious as she was to hear about the deliberate pollution of this river for the sake of profit, she felt deeply relieved that they had finally drilled down into the layer of secrecy that she'd sensed was blanketing this case.

They had some answers, and there would be more to come, as soon as they were face-to-face with the ex-inspector himself.

CHAPTER TWENTY THREE

"Poison," Grace said, as soon as she and Dylan were back in the car and speeding toward Jonesboro. "Poison is at the root of all of this."

Dylan nodded grimly. "Poison from the chemical dumping. More poison from that farm's waste products. It all ended up in the river. Like the victims."

"With their poisoned gags."

Whoever the killer was, it was clear he wanted the victims to suffer in the same way the river had done. An inspector, left jobless after having been involved in these corrupt activities, might easily have had a psychotic break if he was that kind of person to begin with.

So, this raised another question.

"I want to know why Inspector Randall was fired," Grace said. "Who found out? Who fired him? The more of the story we can get, the better. Should we go and ask?"

They'd looked up the ex-inspector's home address, which was in an outlying suburb of Jonesboro, but Grace was now wondering if they should detour past the state offices themselves, first.

Dylan shook his head. "Look, we need to get that information, sure. But it's far more important to get face-to-face with ex-inspector Randall. We can't waste time if he's the one on this killing spree. He could be stalking someone else already."

Grace accepted this was true. Number one priority was to confront the inspector.

"I'll call the offices," she decided. "It's not as effective as getting face-to-face, but it'll save us time."

While Dylan powered along the highway, Grace called the state offices, deciding her best option was to speak to the most senior person in charge.

"Environmental offices, how may I assist you?" a rather bored woman's voice answered.

"FBI Agent Ford," Grace introduced herself. "Is your department head available? It's in connection with a criminal investigation and I need to speak to him urgently. It won't take long."

She hoped she'd gotten the urgency across, and it seemed she'd been lucky because the bored tone had vanished from the woman's voice as she replied, "Hold on, please, Agent. I'll transfer you now."

In another moment, a man's voice said, "Deputy Manager Bryson speaking."

"Mr. Bryson? FBI Agent Ford." Grace reckoned that she was high up enough on the tree to start asking what she needed. "We're investigating the recent string of murders along the river," she said.

"Yes. I've heard about those." Bryson sounded brisk and competent. "You need something from our department?"

"Yes, we need information on a former inspector."

"Who would that be, Agent?" Now he sounded guarded, as if this conversation was straying in a direction he wasn't comfortable with.

"Mr. Randall," Grace said.

Bryson hesitated. "I know he was fired a while ago. I'm not sure how much information I'm authorized to give out."

Grace sighed. People needed to stop being so fearful when the FBI came calling. It was unfortunate that fear was the inevitable response when the long arm of the law reached out. Nobody wanted to be the one who spilled the beans, even in a state department.

"We're aware he was involved in corrupt activities. You'll be telling us nothing new. I just need some background," she said. "I'm not the media. We're not going to publish what you say on the front page, Mr. Bryson. We just need to stop a killer."

Finally, her argument was convincing enough to persuade Bryson to say what he knew.

"What can I tell you?"

"For a start, how did you find out about these activities?"

"There was an article published online, on an environmental blog. It named him."

"Who published the article?" Grace was thinking again about the risk to others.

"We never knew. It was posted anonymously on a blog called GreenSouth. I've no idea who runs it, as there were no contact details; but that didn't matter, because once we had the content, we started digging on our side and we quickly discovered he'd been involved in a lot of corrupt activities. Falsifying water pollution readings, that sort of thing."

"And he was paid off? Who did he receive money from?"

Bryson sighed. "We know who we think was the major culprit, but ma'am, you can put me in jail for a month and I won't say anything out loud, because without proof, I'll get a lawsuit against me faster than you can get the cell locked."

Grace gave an understanding murmur as she heard the words. What Bryson said was true.

"So all we can say is that after a look at the other water readings, re-analyzing the samples, we saw that his records had been off. Way off. Plus, a lifestyle audit showed that he had a large silver Mercedes Benz, which he could not easily have afforded on his state inspector's salary and he could not explain how he'd acquired the money for it. So that was enough. We fired him immediately, and since then, we've been keeping a very close eye on the pollution levels, which were spiking, and they were far too high. It's taken a long time to get them back to levels that aren't actively dangerous. There's still a lot more work to be done."

Grace exchanged a glance with Dylan as he stopped at a light. This was fascinating information.

"The river pollution is no secret," Bryson continued. "There have been complaints for years. Everyone in the state knows about it. It's a major issue and there are a variety of contributing factors. All we can do is try to impose controls to keep it as clean and safe as we can. But there's a lot of room for improvement," he said.

"Did Randall accept your decision?" she asked.

"He was furious about it," Bryson admitted, in a reserved way that told Grace she wasn't getting the full story here. "He tried to oppose our decision, tried to blame the polluters themselves. But the board who'd given the order was very firm and there was no room for negotiation. We do have recourse to a legal team and after a few months, it simmered down. Since then we haven't heard from him."

"Thank you," Grace said. "I think that's all I need, for now, anyway."

"Thank you, Agent," Bryson said. "You can call me if you need anything more. And please, if possible, can you keep this off the record?"

"I'll do that," she promised.

Grace hung up.

So, Randall had been mad. He'd fought the decision. He hadn't accepted it, despite his extravagant purchase of the car. He'd been angry about it and had most likely seen himself as a victim in all of this, a dangerous mindset.

He'd blamed the polluters.

Maybe he'd then decided on payback. Because why should he suffer adverse consequences when the actual polluters had gotten off scot-free? Perhaps that had been his logic.

Randall had a reason to want revenge against those who had fired him. The question was, did he have the capacity for murder? And had he committed these crimes?

They were soon going to find out, because now, they'd arrived at his house.

"This is it," Dylan said, as he pulled up on the side of the quiet road.

Set in a peaceful, ordinary suburb of Jonesboro, the corner property didn't look well-maintained compared to its neighbors. It showed signs of neglect. The yard was overgrown, the windows were dirty. But it looked occupied. A window was open, and on the sill, she could see a couple of beer bottles. Beyond that, in the dim house, a light was on.

It seemed their suspect was home.

Time to confront him.

CHAPTER TWENTY FOUR

As Grace and Dylan walked up to the dilapidated, sad-looking house with the overgrown yard and the battered front door, she had the weird sensation she might actually be glimpsing the owner's damaged mind.

More beer bottles were stacked outside the front door. The doormat was askew. A book, its pages damp and swollen from rain, rested on the steel chair on the porch.

The obvious signs of neglect pointed to someone who could easily have veered into his own delusional reality, she thought, turning her head to Dylan as they stood at that scarred, weathered door.

She knocked.

They waited for a few moments, but there was no answer. Grace knocked again, louder this time, and called out, "Mr. Randall, we need to talk to you. Open up, please."

Silence.

"I think we should take a look around," she said.

She didn't have a good feeling about this. What if there was more going on than they realized? She was beginning to worry that the inspector, too, might have become a victim of whatever revenge games were playing out here.

They walked around together, peeking in the windows.

The kitchen was a mess, with dirty dishes piled up high in the sink. The living room was filled with empty beer bottles and trash scattered on the floor. Still no sign of him there. Perhaps he was out, and that nagging sense of worry in her mind was all for nothing?

They continued prowling around the house, their footsteps rustling in the grass and the overgrown weeds. At the back of the house, under a well-built but not well-maintained shelter, she saw the fancy Mercedes that Bryson from the state offices had told them about. There were a few dents in the bumper and the doors. It was another sign that he was home.

Home, but not answering the door?

Here was another window. What was this?

The bedroom. There was a big double bed, with a scuffed coverlet, which hadn't been made that morning. And something beside it. A rolled up rug?

She caught her breath, just at the same time she heard Dylan mutter in astonishment.

This was no rug. It was a crumpled body.

"No!" she whispered. "What the hell is happening here?"

The man - it looked like a man, as she strained her eyes through the dirty glass - was lying on his side, one arm flung out, his face turned away from them. That was all she could see. The angle was too bad to tell, but he seemed to be motionless.

But the sight of it, the sense of fear and dread that it produced, made her feel sick to her stomach.

"We need to get inside," she said to Dylan, who nodded.

"We need to hustle."

They rushed around to the front door and Grace wrenched the handle down. Locked. Damn it.

"How about the back?" Dylan asked. With a suspected victim inside the home, they were going to have to get in. The only decision was how.

Best case was that the back door was open. Grace ran around the side of the house, stumbling over the uneven ground, anxiety now surging inside her.

Was this man dead? If so, why now and what had happened? What the hell was going on?

The back door was also locked, but unlike the front, this door was flimsier, and it rattled in its frame.

"We can get in this way," Dylan said, and Grace nodded. They needed to, and fast.

She stood aside and Dylan took two steps back, before launching himself at the door. With a lashing kick, his foot slammed against it. Splinters burst from the latch. The door quivered, and then it opened inwards, shuddering on its hinges.

There was no time to waste. They crowded in, racing through the kitchen. There was no stench of decay, she noted, as she rushed down the corridor. Just the sour smell of old food and old dirt, and dusty air. And a strong smell of beer. Another few empty bottles were stacked outside the bedroom door.

Grace rushed in, kneeling down as she reached the slumped man, grabbing his wrist.

It was warm. Flexible. Her mind reeled. This was not what she had expected to touch. He wasn't dead. Now that she was looking more closely, she saw his chest was rising and falling.

A sour smell filled the room. The smell of beer. The carpet was damp. Beer, or else, urine. She wasn't sure, and her nose wrinkled at the possibilities, but the end result was obvious.

Ex-inspector Randall had gone on a massive bender, and the cause of his motionless, prone form was clear. It showed in the bottles and cans surrounding him; it lingered in that stale, stinking air.

Experimentally, she shook his shoulder. And she was rewarded by a grunting sigh.

Bleary, reddened eyes blinked open. Randall was awake.

"What the hell?" His voice was thick and slurred. In an uncoordinated way, he tried to struggle into a sitting position.

Grace and Dylan helped him up, supporting him as he swayed on his feet. It was clear he wasn't going to stay there for long. They managed to shunt him as far as the bed, where his legs buckled again and he folded down.

Grace sighed. This was not what she had expected when they arrived. She thought they were going to uncover some dark and sinister plot, but instead, they found an ex-inspector drunk out of his mind.

It was all he could do to keep his eyes open. In fact, it wasn't all he could do. They slowly closed again, and his eyes rolled back in his head. He let out a sudden, violent snore that made her jump.

At least, this time, he was on the bed and not on the floor. But it was clear they were going to get no sense out of him.

"I'm wondering how long he's been like this," Dylan muttered.

It was an important question. If he'd been on a bender to the extent she was now suspecting, he might have been incapable of committing these crimes.

"How can we find out?" she asked aloud.

"The neighbors, maybe?" Dylan suggested. "If anyone's home, they might know if he's been in or out."

"We're not going to get anywhere here," Grace admitted. The last five minutes had upended her expectations all over again. She was still trying to process the fact that the ex-inspector they had been searching for was lying in front of her, drunk and completely incoherent. He wasn't dead. Her first, worst fears had not been realized.

But there was no way they were getting anything coherent out of this now snoring man.

She stood up, looking quickly through the house, wanting to confirm whether he might have been involved in these crimes, and gotten blind drunk afterward.

Nothing she could find pointed to what she needed. A check in the bedroom and bathroom produced no cotton wool that she could see. There was no smell of chemicals anywhere in the house, and no sign of any toxic substances under the kitchen sink or in the cupboards. Alcohol seemed to be the only substance in use here.

Heading out, Grace felt relieved to be breathing in fresh air again.

"I'll call the police," Dylan said. "Ask them to come and repair his door. Maybe they can also get him some other help." He looked dubiously at the sorry house and the dented car as he dialed. Meanwhile, wanting to do a final check with the neighbors, Grace looked to the left and right. The left-hand house seemed to be occupied. There was a car outside, and she could hear music playing softly from within.

That was the one to try.

The garden gate opened with a squeak and she powered up the path.

As she reached the front door, she could hear voices over the music. People were in the living room.

Grace knocked, and after a moment, the door opened to reveal a middle-aged woman with a shiny red hairdo and gleaming lipstick.

She stared at Grace in surprise.

"FBI Agent Ford," Grace said. "I have some questions I'm hoping you can answer."

"Regarding what?" There was a note of panic in the woman's voice. "We're just playing cards!"

"Regarding your neighbor." She gestured to the house on the right, and understanding dawned in the woman's eyes.

"Oh." There was a wealth of meaning in the word. "Him."

"We've been inside. He's not in a condition to talk to us."

She nodded. "Yeah. He's been like that for a day and a half. He drove home early yesterday morning. Took out half our hedge. We found him in his car at about six a.m. We took him inside, parked his car, and left him there."

"That was very kind of you," Grace said. She nodded grimly.

"I believe in neighborliness," she said, even though it was very clear from the sharp tone of her voice that this was a one-sided endeavor.

"And he hasn't been out of the house since?" Grace asked.

She raised her eyebrows, before turning to the hall table, opening the drawer, and removing a set of keys with a Mercedes star on the keychain.

"Neighborliness extends to saving the lives of others. He's not driving anywhere in this state. When he has sobered up, he can come and ask for his keys back." She gave Grace a grimly satisfied stare.

Grace nodded, feeling grateful that this woman's actions were keeping an inebriated man off the roads – for a while at least. It was good to see that there were still caring people in the world.

"Thank you for your help, and for your responsible actions," she said, before turning to leave. She walked back to Dylan, who had just wrapped up his call.

"Well, it wasn't him." She so badly wanted it to be, but there was no way that this man could have committed that crime.

They were all the way back to the drawing board, and time was ticking on. Three victims, a tenuous link, and still no clear path to the killer.

"There has to be a way forward," she said doggedly.

The clouds were thickening, and the gray day was darkening into drizzle. Grace barely noticed the cold splattering drops on her face and hands as she trailed back to the car.

There was a river, polluted by many sources. Three people who were loosely involved in the pollution, but not necessarily the instigators, had been targeted.

Their killer was not the manager who received the payout to keep quiet. Nor was it the inspector who'd taken bribes to falsify the results.

Even so, the amount of corruption and cover-ups made Grace mad when she thought about them. Before she left, she promised herself, she was going to make sure that company, and its directors, suffered the full wrath of the law for what they had done. No more bribery or escaping the consequences.

But in the meantime she and Dylan were no closer to finding the killer. And there seemed no clear path to follow.

Unless - unless there was something she was missing.

The one angle of the case that she'd briefly heard about, but which they hadn't yet had time to explore further. Now she realized it was the one and only missing link she could think of.

The anonymous whistleblower himself. The owner of the blog that had exposed the inspector.

Perhaps he'd decided to take his own revenge on the polluters.

CHAPTER TWENTY FIVE

He sipped at the glass of water. It looked clear and pure to the naked eye, but only he knew it was not. That water was contaminated. It was tainted with a blend of poisons that he customized according to his mood, and what his mind told him. Tiny droplets of the substances that he infiltrated into the gags were also in this glass.

He knew he needed to do this, out of respect for the man that the poisons had killed. Out of homage to his own son, who had been claimed by the poisons at the young age of twenty.

The water looked so clean, but the chemical reek lingered in the air above it, prickling his nose and eyes as he raised it to his lips again.

He didn't know how fast it was going to kill him, but still, he felt the need to take these drinks. It was part of the balance in life that he should suffer, too. It was all he could do. The only way he could try to feel what his son had felt. To experience what he'd experienced.

He inflicted suffering on others, and they deserved it. He gripped the glass tighter as he thought about that. But he was not immune, and he was also part of the great circle. He was not afraid to suffer himself.

As he lifted the glass, his hands trembled. Well, that was to be expected. They were getting worse. And although it was difficult to assess objectively, he had a strong feeling that his thoughts were becoming more confused.

He couldn't let that happen too fast, because he had to stay sharp, focused on his mission for long enough to complete it, and there were many he wanted to punish. But it was getting harder and harder to control the wanderings of his mind. He found himself drifting off into memories of his son. His athletic build, the muscles no longer slender, as they had been in his teens, but hardening into something more solid. The passionate focus on doing what he loved. His ready grin.

He'd been a good boy. Always independent and hard headed, refusing to listen to advice, believing he was immortal as everyone in their twenties did. But a good son.

The man coughed, the poison water catching in his throat. He put the glass down. It was time to go out. Time had fled away with him, he realized, startled. He'd thought he had an hour to spare, but now, there were only a few short minutes before he needed to be in place.

Maybe he shouldn't have taken that drink; perhaps it would not have hurt to skip the ritual for just one day. But no. It was important. He had forced himself to do it every day for months now, and he would keep doing it. He would!

He turned, grasped the bag with the items he needed, and headed to the door.

Closing it behind him, he saw his neighbor approaching, making her careful way up the garden path, holding an umbrella over her gray head because a cold, spattering drizzle was falling.

That was good. Wet mud would help cover his tracks.

"Good morning," she greeted him. Then the smile vanished as she looked at him more closely. "You look pale. Are you okay?"

He forced a smile of his own, hoping to appear as normal as possible. The last thing he wanted was for her to think something was wrong.

"Just a stomach flu. Nothing to worry about."

He shifted the bag in his hand, hoping to hurry the conversation along. He had important work to do, and he couldn't afford to be late.

"You should take care of yourself," she said, her voice softening with concern. "Maybe you should go see a doctor?"

He shook his head. No way would he go to a doctor now. Blood tests, at this time, would surely pick up things that could seal his fate. "I'll be fine," he said, before sidestepping her and heading down the path. He could hear her calling out to him, but he didn't turn back. He was already late, and needed to get where he was going.

He was now wondering if she was really so innocent. He'd thought so, but now it seemed he might be wrong.

If she kept asking questions and acting so concerned, he would have to kill her, too. That, he knew. It would be a pre-emptive strike, because if she was going to inform the authorities about him, she was as dangerous as the polluters themselves.

The fog in his mind cleared as he got into his car. Strangely, it seemed to do that after he'd drunk from his poisoned glass, although it always felt just a little worse when it descended again.

For now, though, driving was easier than it had been the last time he went out.

The road seemed clearer, despite the misty rain that was blanketing the area. He switched on the windshield wipers, and watched as they rhythmically flicked it away.

His destination was an important one. This was the home of the next victim, and he was eager to see him die.

The man owned a car service dealership that for years - as he'd discovered - had been dumping used engine oil into a stream that fed the river.

The company had been taken over after the last owner had died, and he believed that the new owner had put an immediate stop to the practice, but it was too little, too late.

If you inherited poison, then you had to pay. That was his motto.

Taking down those who had been the bringers of death, those who had caused pain and suffering, was a calling he was proud of. Somebody had to take action and make them atone for what they had done.

This should go smoothly if he judged it right. His research had shown that there was a time during the day when this man was alone, and that was for an hour or two in the mornings, when his assistant was out, test driving or delivering cars.

He'd have to be very careful, because the mists were lowering again and making it difficult to see. As he parked two blocks down, he decided to go there on foot. If he was sure that his target was alone, then he'd come back in a car.

He couldn't afford to mess this up. He had to get this next target, to identify all the miscreants who had contributed to this. And then, he would spread the net wider. There were others who needed to pay, too.

This was just the start.

Poison swirled through his mind as he got out of the car and walked toward the workshop.

The taste still hung in his mouth as he strode toward the entrance. A sour, bitter reek that scoured his tongue and flavored his breath.

But revenge - oh, he knew from experience that every time this happened, the taste in his mouth would change.

Then, it became so sweet.

CHAPTER TWENTY SIX

"So, we need to find this blogger." Grace felt determined that this, her last possible lead with a clear motive for the crimes, was going to come through. “But he’s anonymous. All we have is the site name, GreenSouth.”

They were holed up together in the closest police station, where they'd borrowed a room to set up their laptops and to take a look at the website that the state official had told them about.

"I'm going to get hold of Zach right now, and see if the IT techs can help us," Dylan said, picking up his phone. He called, listened, and then said, "Okay. In ten, then." He turned to Grace. "He's wrapping up a meeting and will call me back as soon as he's walked out."

Who ran this blog, and where was that person now?

It was most definitely a homemade site. Nothing about it was professional, from the garish green color scheme to the clashing design elements. However, Grace did acknowledge, once you started reading the blog posts, it was difficult to stop.

Grace scrolled through the homepage, scanning for any clues as to who was behind it. The site was strongly focused on environmental issues, and the stance was militant about bringing punishment to those who had destroyed 'Mother Earth,' as the writer called it.

Although well written, and reasonably coherent, the articles had no filter, and straight after a scientific explanation of how agricultural runoff polluted the water and created dead zones downstream, which opened Grace’s eyes to the logistics of the process, there was a passionate call for all offenders to be tied up and thrown into the river to face the consequences of their actions.

Her eyebrows rose as she read that.

Dylan leaned over her shoulder, reading the screen. "This guy sounds like he's gone overboard in his desire for payback," he said. "This is exactly the mentality we've been looking for."

Grace nodded. "You can see he is personally invested in what's happening. This is someone who lives his mission."

And how far had it taken him, she wondered?

She clicked on the "About" page yet again, wondering if she'd pick up something new this time that she'd missed, but there was no information on the creator or the team behind the site. There were only instructions on how to make payment, via bitcoin, if you 'supported the good work and wanted it to continue.' There was no address, no name attached to this blog, not even any background on who the writer was.

For this, they were going to need the full investigative might of the FBI.

Dylan's phone rang, and he grabbed it up. It was Zach, returning the call.

"We have a lead," Dylan told their boss. "But we can't get to him. It's an anonymous blog and we need the tech department's help in tracking it."

"What's the address? And why do you suspect this person?" Dylan turned the phone to speaker and Zach's voice, sharp and focused, filled the small office.

Grace quickly filled Zach in on what they had discovered. "The blogger, who runs the site GreenSouth, might be the one behind the killings. He was the whistleblower who exposed the corrupt inspector by writing an article, and he seems to be militant about punishing people who have harmed the environment. Drowning and gagging are mentioned."

"I'm putting the IT department onto that right now. We'll see what we can get." Zach paused, then added, "I'm heading into a meeting at one p.m. with the director. He's aware of these killings. Very aware."

There was a wealth of meaning in his tone, and Grace exchanged an uneasy glance with Dylan. This task force was new. A failure, so early on in their existence, would not look good on their record - and the director would be scrutinizing that closely.

By one p.m. today, they needed a breakthrough. They needed a suspect in custody. And she was hopeful that this person was going to be their guy, if they could locate him. The rants on the site were practically a profile of the killer.

Militant. Passionate. A willingness to go to any lengths.

"I'll let you know as soon as we have something," Zach promised, before hanging up.

Grace knew the IT department would be doing their part, tracking the IP address, finding out who was behind the blog. But there were things that she and Dylan could do, too, while they waited.

Grace scoured the web. She wasn't an IT expert but she was a good researcher. She was sharp-eyed and fast, and if there was a mention of him, hidden away anywhere online, she hoped that she would find it.

" GreenSouth. Who are you? Where are you?"

There were a few mentions of the blog online. Other people were also curious about the owner. She saw a discussion group that theorized about who he was, without any real answers. Some other news sites linked to the blog as a resource.

Information from this blog, it seemed, was a reliable source, when it didn't stray into the realm of punishing the environmental offenders.

But nobody seemed to know who he was.

Silence fell in the office, interrupted only by the tapping of keys as Grace and Dylan tried their best to root out this anonymous eco-warrior's identity. But without success.

When Dylan's phone rang again, it felt as if this onerous responsibility had finally been lifted from them. Only, as Dylan spoke, Grace realized it wasn't turning out that way.

"Okay," he said. "Okay. I understand. We'll keep looking on our side."

He hung up, looking frustrated. "Zach is getting nothing. The IP address is proving difficult to track. The blog is run from a VPN, or virtual private network, which is making it more difficult. They're trying other ways, and they think they can do it, but it'll take time."

They didn't have time. Feeling stressed by their lack of progress, Grace turned back to the research, knowing that where IT was delayed, her own basic skills were now all that they had.

Perhaps the articles themselves could give a clue, she wondered.

That writing. The format of the pieces. Why were they so readable? There was something about their structure that was ringing a bell with her. Abandoning her search, she went back to the blog itself.

The way those posts were written, the grammatical correctness.

"You know what?" she said to Dylan. "I think this writer is a trained journalist. I'm going to call the local news sites, and ask them if they have any idea who he is. Perhaps one of them has an idea."

"Now that's a good angle," Dylan agreed.

There were three local news sites that focused on reporting the news in this part of the world. Two were in Arkansas and one was in Tennessee. A local site would be best, Grace decided, although there were a few others that might also be helpful.

She started with the first site in Arkansas, while Dylan took the Tennessee news and information site.

Grace made a call, introduced herself as FBI, and was soon speaking to the senior editor.

"Do you have any idea who the writer of GreenSouth is?"

There was a thoughtful silence.

"Ma'am, I can't tell you that," the man said. There was something in his voice, though, that made her press further.

"No ideas? Even to give the FBI a lead?" she questioned.

"Not to speak badly of the opposition, of course. But I have always wondered, personally, if he might have been one of the journalists from the other news site in our area, the Arkansas Community Updater. I know they had a staff turnover recently, soon after the time that blog started out."

"Thank you," she said.

Feeling encouraged by this, she called the Arkansas Community Updater and asked to speak to the editor.

A few minutes, and a few explanations, later, she was put through to a deep voiced man with a slow, deliberate way of speaking.

This time, after introducing herself, she phrased her question differently.

"I believe you had a staff turnover recently and a couple of journalists left. Do you have their names?"

It was an easy question. She didn't foresee a problem in answering it. But there was one.

"I'm sorry. I'm not willing to disclose that information," the editor said after a thoughtful pause. "Our staff records are kept private, and we don't share the reasons why our journalists move on."

"But -" Grace began.

She was speaking to a dead line. He'd hung up on her.

"Well! Now that is rude! And, Mister-one-word-a-minute, it's telling me there's something weird going on here," she grumbled.

Now feeling as if she was preparing for battle, she began doing her own research, delving into the news archives and noting down who the writers were. Particularly those who'd focused on environmental issues.

As she scrolled through the archives, one name kept coming up over and over. Jonas Sudbury. He'd been a prolific writer of environmental stories, but she couldn't find any recent articles under his name. It seemed that, a year or so ago, he'd stopped writing for the

Arkansas Community Updater, and she couldn't find any other articles under his name.

She scrolled through one of his historic articles and to her, the journalistic style seemed similar. The same clear writing, and the same vicious undertone when talking about offenders.

"Look here."

Dylan was off the phone after another fruitless call to the statewide news sites, and she showed him what she'd found.

He raised his eyebrows. "Grace, look at the timeline. GreenSouth was started about a year ago. That exposé was one of the first articles. He might have been fired because of it. Did the media site refuse to publish it, and did he get into trouble? Did this corruption spread even further?"

Grace considered his words. She liked them. A lot.

"I think we've got him," she said.

CHAPTER TWENTY SEVEN

What they needed now were two things they didn't have. A phone number for Jonas Sudbury, and a way of tracking it.

Grace called Zach back. This time, she hoped, they'd get a better result from the FBI's resources.

"Grace? I'm about to go into the meeting, but if you need help, I'll delay it," her boss answered, his voice taut.

She could visualize him, in the Minnesota office she knew so well, pacing up and down on the tiled floor outside the meeting room. That was the way he liked to prepare before difficult confrontations, and she knew that with these unsolved crimes, this was going to be difficult.

"We've found him, I think. At any rate, it's a very strong suspect. It looks like he's an ex-journalist. Name of Jonas Sudbury."

"You have an address?"

"I have an old address," Grace said. "We just looked it up. It seems that Sudbury sold his house after he was fired, and he bought a campervan. We have the license plate."

"Okay?" Zach sounded hopeful.

"But of course, the vehicle could be anywhere. We need a phone number for him, and if possible, a cellphone GPS tracker. Then we can find him. I'm sure of it."

She exchanged an excited glance with Dylan. They were close now.

"I'm going to get this organized. Right away." She heard him speaking to someone else. "Tell the director I'll be a few minutes late. I need to take urgent action on this serial case."

Then, she heard his footsteps hurrying back into the main office, which she could also visualize. She could sense the surge of excitement that filled the room as he broke the news that the task force was hot on the killer's heels.

Familiar voices came faintly through the phone, the sounds of her old team members, as they researched the cellphone number linked to this man and got a tracker set up on it.

"It's almost done," Zach said. "We're waiting for a connection. You got that iPad ready? I'm going to link it straight up so you can see." He paused. "Good luck."

"We'll do our best," Grace promised, turning to the iPad and watching it, feeling like a lion tracking its prey.

The tracker beeped, and a location popped up on the screen.

"He's right there! Near the river!" Dylan's voice was sharp.

The red pin drop was unmistakable. Their target was in the area, and he was at a place on the river that was in between the two most recent dumping grounds.

Now, the chase was on.

*

Fifteen minutes later, with the sun now peeking out from behind the heavy morning cloud, Grace and Dylan sped down the bumpy track to the river's edge. Their car bounced and jolted over the ruts in the road, and Grace braced her feet against the floor, feeling intent that this killer was now in their sights.

There was the campervan. A humble, gray vehicle, it was parked in a grassy spot under a tree. Dylan hit the brakes and Grace climbed out, her feet squelching in the muddy ground and her hand moving automatically to the grip of her gun for a moment as she stared at the campervan.

They moved toward it.

It was very quiet. The soft rippling of the river provided a background noise that was more threatening than lulling now that she knew the way the communities had misused this water, creating in somebody's mind a terrifying need for revenge.

Dylan raised his hand and hammered on the door.

Silence.

He tried the door, but it was locked.

In the window, on the narrow sill, Grace saw a discarded pair of binoculars. This man had been on the lookout. Had he seen them?

She turned her gaze to the muddy pathway going down to the river. And now, she could see heavy, booted footprints leading away from the door and following the track in that direction.

"He's gone there," she said, pointing. The tracks only went one way. There were no returning footprints in the fresh mud.

They turned away from the campervan and followed the tracks, but as they went, Grace began to realize something.

These footprints were too far apart for a man to have made them by walking. These were the fresh, deep, hurried footprints of a running man.

An unwelcome realization dawned. He'd been watching, and he'd seen them. And he'd fled.

She and Dylan had exactly the same thought at the same time. They both broke into a run, sprinting along the sodden track, following those deep imprints along the winding trail that led steeply down to the river - to a convenient access point into the waters - and then veered right, heading through thick brush along its banks.

The river rushed by on her left, its waters dark and turbulent. The trees on her right formed a dense, thorny barrier that scratched at her arms and legs as she plowed her way through, tracking those prints.

And then, she saw him. A tall, broad shouldered man in a camouflage coat, running hard along the trail. His legs moved forward.

"Stop! FBI! Jonas Sudbury, stop!" she yelled.

She knew he'd heard. But if anything, he ran faster.

Jonas Sudbury was now in sight, and Grace could see him glancing back over his shoulder, gauging his pursuers' distance. She saw fear in his thickly bearded face.

She sped up, needing to close that distance, because he was running at a frantic pace, and she felt sure that he was realizing the consequences of his actions.

Dylan was running behind her, but Grace knew that he was still feeling his knee and that the pain and weakness of that injury were affecting his speed. This takedown was up to her.

Ahead, Jonas slipped in the mud, losing his footing and giving Grace what she needed - a chance to get closer. She took it, giving it everything she had, using her voice as well as her presence to threaten this man.

"FBI! You'll be in more trouble if you keep running! Stop! This is an order!" she yelled.

But it was clear that Jonas had no intention of stopping. Instead, he veered to the right, plunging into the thick overgrowth of trees.

"Hey! Wait!" she shouted. What was he doing and why had he headed that way? Did he have a plan in mind, or had he been heading deliberately to a secret bolt hole? She'd thought that there was nowhere to hide along this muddy river path, and that it would be a simple case of outrunning him, relying on her stamina to give her the edge.

Now, she was rethinking that, with a clench of fear. He had been two steps ahead, all along.

Grace pounded up to the place where he'd gone, but to her consternation, when she arrived, there was no sign of him.

The path was so waterlogged she couldn't see where the footprints ended, and nor could she see a place where he'd broken through the foliage.

Their strong suspect had disappeared in the blink of an eye.

CHAPTER TWENTY EIGHT

Think, Grace told herself. This is overgrown, riverside terrain, and he couldn't just have vanished. No way could he have disappeared without a trace.

She tried to still her own breathing. Tried her best to be quiet. Listened, her ears straining, her eyes moving over the terrain as she tried to attune herself to its nuances. Being in unfamiliar territory was no excuse for missing a detail. She needed to adapt her eyes.

Was that a flicker of movement in the bushes there? The crack of a stick? She looked closer. She peered into the undergrowth. Dylan had fallen far behind and it was now up to her.

Now, finally, her senses were cooperating with her and she was seeing the patterns in between the leaves. The puzzle pieces were slotting together. It had taken a while, but now, it was there.

Grace moved forward, intent on her target.

The pattern completed itself, moving away from the background, and there he was. He'd taken cover under a thick, bushy plant and was crouched down, his jacket blending in almost perfectly, only the rapid rise and fall of his shoulders giving any indication that a human was hiding here.

"Jonas Sudbury, this is the FBI. Come out now with your hands up," she said firmly.

There was no response, only the sound of the rushing river and the rustling of leaves in the wind.

Grace took another step closer, and suddenly Jonas sprang up from his hiding spot, lunging toward her.

"Watch it!" From the bend in the path, she heard Dylan shout in warning as their target erupted from his hiding place.

“No! Not the police!”

He launched himself, more than two hundred pounds of heavy, desperate weight on a collision course with her.

Her training kicked in, and she managed to duck away, twisting sideways to avoid being knocked right off her feet as he plowed toward her. She got out of his path, but now she needed to act, because she was not going to let him escape. Surprise attacks could only go so far, Grace thought grimly, as she made a grab for his arm and caught his sleeve.

Then, she used his own speed against him, yanking him forward and sideways and sticking out her foot to trip him up, so that his own momentum worked against him, and he fell to his knees with a cry.

And then, Dylan was on the scene, lunging forward with a gasp as his bad leg buckled under him. But he was close enough to grab Jonas's other arm and twist it up behind his back.

"You're coming in. Now," he muttered breathlessly. "No more sneak attacks. That's over. And we want answers."

*

This time, they were going to get the truth from their suspect.

Grace promised herself that, as she stood outside the interview room preparing for the interrogation of Jonas Sudbury.

They'd let him wait in here for an hour, alone. They'd done that for two reasons. First, they wanted him to have some time to stew, to think about his actions, and the consequences. Grace had wanted to give him longer, but she knew how pressured the time was with their boss in this critical top level meeting.

Second, it allowed the forensic team to start searching his RV, where Grace hoped more evidence would be found. If anything was uncovered, it could help them with their interrogation, so the timing had been important here.

It was two p.m. and the director's meeting would be under way in Minnesota. Zach would be discreetly checking his phone, hoping for an update, looking for the news which would prove to him, and to the director, that the task force was effectively fighting crime in the problematic Mississippi River area.

"Let's go do this," she said to Dylan.

She opened the door.

Roughly cleaned up from the mud and dirt that had coated him after the takedown, Jonas sat in the chair, his hands cuffed to the table. He looked up at them with a defiant glower.

Keeping calm, Grace stepped forward, her eyes locking onto his.

"Mr. Sudbury, do you know why you're here?" she asked, sitting down.

Jonas stared at her with aggression in his eyes. "I'm an innocent man! I've done nothing wrong. You clearly think I have, so why don't you tell me why I'm here, Agent?" he replied.

"Your blog. GreenSouth."

"What about it?"

"You've been crusading against people who've been polluting the river. How far did you take it?"

Jonas stared at them angrily. "Oh, that's what this is about? You're saying it's okay for the river to be poisoned and polluted by unscrupulous profiteers? I did what I had to do to protect the environment. I've been trying to save this river for years, but no one would listen."

"What did you do, Jonas?" Grace asked.

He shrugged. "You've read my blog. You can read, I take it, even though you're law enforcement?" His tone was sour with mockery.

Grace didn't even notice that insult. She was too focused on his body language, his demeanor, and figuring out the reasons why he was saying this. Was he confessing? Hinting to something?

"So you're admitting to certain actions?" she asked.

Jonas smirked. "I'm not admitting to anything. I'm just saying that sometimes the ends justify the means."

"What means did you use?"

He grinned, a mirthless, cold expression. "It's all about exposing people. I know a lot."

"You took it further, didn't you?"

He nodded. "Of course I did! Who wouldn't? I enjoyed every minute of what I did! After all, I was unfairly fired. I wanted to publish the story, but my bosses delayed, and then they delayed again, and then they gave me an outright no, they said they couldn't do it, they couldn't cause damage to a local business that way, when so many people from the area were employed there. And soon after that, they were going on expensive vacations and upgrading their cars." He looked at her meaningfully. “You get me? Corrupt, one and all.”

“So what did you do?” Grace asked.

“I published it anyway on my blog. They knew it was me of course. I was the only one who had the facts, so they fired me. They were probably told to by Lewes Inc. who are their real bosses. But it's okay. I made plans to destroy that toxic company, plans that are in progress now.”

"Did that involve killing three individuals?"

Now, Jonas looked cagier.

"I'm not going to confess to anything like that. I'm not stupid, Agent. I'll taunt you for as long as there are hours in the day, because the police have never been there for me, and I have utter contempt for you. All this is material for a future blog post. My wrongful arrest, this interrogation, and whatever follows. But a forced confession is a different matter. It's a no from me on that, and it always will be."

He gazed at the ceiling, whistling softly to himself as Dylan frowned.

Grace's phone buzzed, and while Dylan was pressuring Jonas for more details, she glanced down at the screen.

It was a text from the forensic team who were working at the campervan. Had they found information? Quickly, she opened it.

"We have found something. Call me when you can," the message read.

Grace's heart sped up. Evidence was the missing link, and if they got it, she knew that this case would be signed and sealed. They had a suspect who was refusing to incriminate himself. Fair enough. Most suspects did exactly that when arrested, and that was why evidence was so all-important.

Obtaining that evidence would be all they needed. Even if he didn't confess, it would hopefully be sufficient when it came to trial. But Grace hoped for more. She had seen how sometimes, when faced with the evidence that finally buried them, suspects would change their tack and confess freely to what they'd done. Sometimes, they would even brag about it, as if the evidence finally gave them permission to take that step.

She hoped that they could nail Jonas with what forensics had found.

Quickly, she left the interview room, to find out what it was.

CHAPTER TWENTY NINE

"What have you found?" Grace asked the forensic officer the crucial question as soon as the call connected.

"We've found a big storage shelf with sealed jars of water. They appear to contain dilutions of toxic substances," the officer said. "At any rate, that's what the labels say. Mercury, benzene, organic phosphorus, and a few others."

This was it. Grace gripped the phone harder. This was exactly what they needed to connect Jonas to the murders and the pollution of the river.

"We need those seized. Urgently," she emphasized.

"We're going to bring the containers in and we'll get them tested to confirm the contents," he said.

“Anything resembling a gag? Any of the rope that the killer uses?”

“Nothing like that. Just the jars.”

But the jars were enough. Surely?

As she thanked him and hung up the phone, Grace felt a wave of relief wash over her. After chasing leads and coming up against dead ends, they finally had some of what they needed to tie Jonas to the murders She hurried back into the interrogation room, where Dylan was still grilling Jonas.

"Mr. Sudbury, we have some new evidence to add to our case," she said. She felt vindicated as she saw the astonishment in his eyes.

"You can't possibly have any evidence against me!"

"We've searched your motor home," she said. "We've found water samples that contain dilutions of toxic substances. I'm sure you know how that's been used."

Staring challengingly at him, she hadn't known what to expect when she said that, but she'd never expected the reaction that followed.

"No!" He shouted the word in horror. "No, no, you can’t do that!" He banged his fists on the table, rattling the cuffs, his face contorted with anxiety. "I didn't mean for it to go this far. I just wanted to protect the river. I wanted to show you that I wouldn't cave to your pressure, no matter what!"

"What are you saying?" she asked, puzzled by this extreme reaction, but he didn't answer her directly. Instead, his diatribe continued.

"I don't trust you! I won't, I How can I? You always side with the powerful people. There's nobody more bent than a cop. You don't care about the ordinary guys, the ones who are fighting for the truth. And now you're going to prevent me from doing what I need to do, to save my own reputation. My home is private! Leave those samples alone!"

He looked like a trapped animal, his gaze darting around the room as if searching for a way out.

Grace stared at him in disbelief. This man was admitting that he had poison samples in his possession, and now he was begging them to leave the evidence alone? It didn't make sense. But then again, neither did the murders he was suspected of committing.

Was he genuinely remorseful for what he had done or was it just a ploy to save his own skin? Either way, the evidence spoke for itself. They had found jars of water mixed with toxic substances in his motor home, and the labels matched the chemicals found in the gags. There was no denying his involvement now.

Except then, he spoke again.

"I'm going to have to trust you, aren't I?" he asked, as if the thought was too horrific to contemplate. "Trust the police! I'm going to have to, because of what you've done."

Grace stared at him in utter puzzlement. She had no idea if he was genuinely distressed, or if he was a fantastically skilled actor who was drawing them into deception in a last attempt to save himself.

Beside her, Dylan was shaking his head in confusion.

"Look, Mr. Sudbury, as it stands, you're in serious trouble. And if you have an argument you need to give us, then explain yourself," he said.

He sighed, rattling his cuffs. "Any chance you can let me out of these? I keep panicking inside them," he said.

"No!" Dylan said, at exactly the same time that Grace moved forward. She stopped, glanced at him. He gave her a warning frown, consternation written all over his face.

"I think it will be okay to compromise," she mouthed to him. Then, she leaned over and unlocked their suspect's right wrist.

"You're not getting out of both of them. But I will let you out of one cuff. We're meeting you halfway on this. Now, it's your chance to do the same," she challenged him.

He raised a shaking hand and rubbed his forehead, rubbed his eyes, wiped his nose on his sleeve, and shook out his arm as if it had been in pain.

"Please, don't break those jars, or empty them, or mess them up," he said. "I've been collecting those water samples for many months. I started a couple of years ago, when I got some phone calls from locals to say strange things were happening, that they'd seen a pipe running into the river, that the water smelled bad, that farmers were also jumping on the bandwagon and dumping their waste inside because now it was 'polluted anyway.' I want to expose that damned company and destroy them."

"Which company?" Grace asked, just for clarity.

"Lewes Inc., of course! They paid off my bosses at the media company. They were the reason that story didn't run. So I published it anonymously and then I got fired. I got threats from them, too. I've kept those. You'll find them in my home. I'm building up a whole stack of evidence against them. But I'm not the killer. I don't know who's been killing these people and dumping those bodies at the swimming and fishing access points, but I've followed the reports and kept track of it, because I don't want him to come for me."

"You're saying the killer's not you? Who is he, then?"Dylan challenged.

"How should I know? Some psycho! But he might have his reasons. I know there were a few incidents over the past couple of years. People called to tell me about it, before I was fired, and even after. There were a few folks who got sick from swimming in that polluted river. I know. I have hospital sources. They kept it quiet because where do you publish things when the local press has been corrupted? Maybe someone got sick, and decided it was payback time."

He stared at them triumphantly.

"Give us a moment," Grace said.

She stood, and walked out of the interview room, with Dylan following.

"He's lying, I'm telling you," Dylan said, as soon as the door had closed.

Grace shook her head. "He might be, but what if he's not? What if he's telling the truth, and the killer's still out there?" She paused, feeling frazzled. "One of the things he said, about those access points. I've just realized that it's correct. Every one of those access points where bodies have been dumped, are ones that a swimmer could use, if the river wasn't so polluted. Remember, we even saw the old signage. Now I'm realizing it. Perhaps that's why this killer is choosing those sites. It's part of the message he's sending out. Dylan, I'm worried now that he's still out there. That this is going to get worse. And then, it'll be on our watch, because we persisted in following the wrong lead."

Dylan frowned. "I don't think you're right. But maybe we should check?"

"I'll tell you what. We can look in the missing persons reports again and see if anyone has been reported missing in the area today. If it looks like it might be suspicious, then that will give us a lead. Just as a start."

"Good idea. Let's go and do that," he agreed, but in a tone that told Grace he still wasn't convinced.

They headed to the office next door. As they logged into the latest crime reports, Grace couldn't believe how anxious she felt. The problem was that the journalist's story made logical sense. Once he'd stopped being so fearful, and distrusting the police, she could see that he was able to explain himself clearly.

Would this killer be so logical? That, she didn't know.

And then, scrolling his mouse down the list, Dylan drew in a sharp breath.

"Uh-oh," he said.

"What is it?" Grace leaned forward.

"Nolan Carruthers has just been reported missing. He owns a motor repair company in a town in northern Arkansas, bordering the river. His assistant went out for a test drive, and when he came back, he said his boss had vanished. Car and phone were still there, but the man was gone." He looked more closely. "He disappeared between two and three hours ago. We had Jonas in custody by then! So he couldn't have taken him."

"Motor repairs. Engine oil," Grace said. "A known polluter of water. It's him, Dylan. I know it is. He's done it again."

"We can't be sure. All we know is that a man who might have been someone the killer would target, is missing."

"We have to take this seriously!" Grace knew her eyes were blazing as she turned to face him. "Even if it's the biggest waste of time. I felt that Jonas's argument was persuasive. I could understand why he had those jars there. He trusted us, and now, we have to trust him. At least, until we've ruled out that the real killer has taken Nolan Carruthers."

"And how do you want to go ahead then?" At least Dylan sounded more open to the idea now.

"He's using swimmer's access points into the river. We know the areas he's operating in. There are a limited number of places he can be. If he’s going to dump a victim, then for sure, it’ll be soon after dark. So, we need to get a team together, monitor those points, and catch him in the act."

CHAPTER THIRTY

He knew time was running out for what he needed to do. The mists were closing in, but he welcomed them, because he knew that although they took from him, they also gave him the power he needed. He was going to kill this new victim, this polluter.

And then, he was going to go back home, and knock on his elderly neighbor's door. He didn’t know how he’d kill her. Perhaps he’d take her to the river, too. Or maybe just drown her in the bathtub.

It was what she deserved. Her interfering words were troubling his mind, and it was time to put a stop to them.

See a doctor? The dealer of death would see no doctors. In fact, he was now thinking that he didn't need any intervention. He thought the time might come when he started being able to resist the poison he took. After all, at the crucial time, he seemed to be able to draw on the extreme reserves of power he needed.

Either way, it was clear, the more quickly he killed now, the better. It would refill his almost empty cup.

The juddering ride, with the poison soaked gag, was now in progress. The head rush as he'd grabbed his latest victim had been one of the most extreme moments of his life. Now, he was trussed and gagged in the trunk, the poisons filtering into his system to sicken and weaken him.

He'd been fair here, too.

This man had not contributed as much to his son's demise. Those toxins could not have killed alone, though they had polluted. For that reason, he had been sparing in his use of poison as he'd soaked the gag. It was the river itself that would kill this one, which seemed like perfect justice. After all procuring the poisons was difficult, and he didn’t want to run out when he had so many that must die.

As the car came to a stop by the river, he took a deep breath and stepped out. He opened the trunk and dragged the man out, his body limp and helpless.

He would not be helpless for long. This victim was a strong, tough guy. Luckily he'd been able to surprise him completely while he'd been bent over a car’s open hood, busy hammering an engine pipe into shape. The banging noise had completely camouflaged his footsteps. The triumph he felt as he remembered that moment gave him the strength he needed now to lift him easily.

Or perhaps it was the river that imbued him with that power.

He shouldered the man, letting out a grunt of effort, but bearing the weight, feeling his boots sink into the mud. It didn't matter. At some stage, before the mists had gotten too thick, he'd glued bigger soles onto the bottoms of those boots. If any prints were left, the police would be hunting a giant. Not him. Strong though he was, he wasn't even six feet tall. It was the burning drive within him that motivated him to do what he did.

He walked towards the riverbank, glancing at the horizon where the merest trace of fiery light remained. In a moment it would be dark.

By the time he had completed his ritual, he knew night would have fallen. The burial and also the words he spoke were important. He couldn’t skip that step, although he usually waited until later in the evening to do it.

This time, though, he was pressed, because he needed to get back and deal with his neighbor. He had a lot to do tonight.

He had chosen his spot carefully. This particular stretch of the river was isolated and quiet, with no swimmers or boaters in sight, though it was one of their entry points. An old sign, nailed to a tree, attested to a time when the river had been cleaner. It was a spot he had scouted before and was confident in his knowledge of the terrain.

The man's body was now slung over his shoulder as he made his way carefully down the embankment towards the water's edge. The river was cold and murky, and he could sense it was in an evil mood. The dark waters lapped over his feet as he dumped the man down. His trussed victim struggled weakly, but he ignored him, and began the work of digging.

He did it with his hands and feet, no tools needed. All he had to do was scoop out a resting place in that muddy bed close to the water. It didn't take long. Maybe half an hour. By the time he’d finished it was completely dark, as his prisoner, half conscious, lay in the shallows. The mists made time pass faster so that it felt like the blink of an eye.

And then, it was time to place him there, so that the water could cover him.

Exhausted but elated, he picked him up and dumped him in the muddy shallows. The river had moods and rhythms and he knew them well because he had learned them. In an hour, as the wind increased and the river swelled from the rains upstream, the waters would be a foot higher and the man's face would be long covered. Already weak, he would soon be dead.

But time, now, to punish him. He saw his eyes, wide and terrified, above the poison gag that he wished he'd made stronger.

He needed to make sure that the man suffered for what he had done to his son. The dealer of death felt a surge of anger as he thought about the pain his son had gone through before he died.

He'd been a headstrong young man always, in love with swimming, refusing to listen to the warning signs of pollution, ignoring the cautions and the notices, believing he was stronger. But days, weeks, months of spending time in that river at its worst, with the illegal pollution, had taken its toll and he'd sickened. He'd passed out in the water and it had gotten into his lungs and ultimately, it had been a combination of factors that had killed him in the hospital.

Pneumonia was what they'd written on the death certificate, but he knew it had really been the poisons.

Desperate for answers, he'd searched out the culprits, and this man's business was one.

"You were the source of the poison," he hissed, feeling his own throat raw. "You were death; you were destruction. But I am destroying you. You had no right to pollute those waters, to take lives, to destroy what you never owned. So I am destroying you!"

Impassioned, he continued his hoarse diatribe until he could no longer speak, until the words were husking out of his throat. His hands had started shaking again, worse than ever. His head was spinning. But still he felt capable of drawing on a dreadful, killing strength.

Then he turned and strode up the muddy bank, feeling spent.

A sense of triumph filled him. He'd been able to send another evil soul to its punishment and he'd done so without being seen.

Or had he? As he trudged along the pathway leading back to his car, he saw a flashlight. Someone else was here.

Instinctively he turned his face away, but the light followed him, bright and blazing, and awakening all his fears as it drew near.

"Excuse me!" a voice shouted. "Please, sir! May I ask your name?"

It was the police. He knew it immediately from that tone. They were looking, searching, and his panic surged.

Pretend to be who you aren't, a voice hissed inside his head. There's only one of them there. One, who needs to be punished and drowned.

Knowing this was his only chance to escape, he hunched his shoulders. He staggered, and he coughed.

Feigning weakness would lure this person in and then he would strike.

CHAPTER THIRTY ONE

"We have to map this area out and deploy patrols at every swimming and boating access point!"

Frantically, because there was no time left and a killer to catch, Grace pored over the large scale maps of the area that she'd called up on her screen.

Meanwhile, she could hear Dylan's voice in the lobby, as he gave orders to call other precincts, to get backup involved and head out to the river, as many officers as possible. His first phone call, on the way to the lobby, had been to Detective Stoll.

Then, Dylan would have to call the Tennessee police, and set up exactly the same protocols on that side of the river. It was a huge exercise, and there were numerous points to cover. They might not be able to reach all of them. How far north and south were they going to spread their net?

Knowing that estimating this incorrectly would mean a potential death, she agonized over the map, looking at the points so far, trying to estimate what the outer borders of his zone would be.

She feared, with darkness setting in and with so many points where people could boat or swim, that it was going to be a futile exercise. But they had to try.

Dylan limped back in with a paper copy of the map, wincing as his knee twisted under him, but ignoring the pain and getting onto the radio. As he got agreement from the various teams, he marked out different areas. But, in two states where resources were thinly stretched and space was vast, that was a difficult task.

She thought that he'd done an amazing job. She'd listened to him, cheerful and positive, encouraging the branches to make plans and rally around. Even Detective Stoll had sounded enthused as he'd agreed to place four teams at the closest entry points.

As he got confirmation, Dylan was placing pin drops on the map with each team that agreed to participate. More and more of the entry points were being covered.

And finally, there were only three left. They were the most southerly points on the Arkansas side. Fairly close together, but she wasn't sure if they were too far south for the killer to want to use them.

"We don't have anyone for those? Do you think we need to include them?"

Dylan shook his head. "Every available officer has been deployed. I think those points are too far south. But if you like, you and I could check them?"

"Let's do that," she agreed, feeling glad that they could take action and not have to sit in the office and watch.

It was a still, cold evening, and a light rain was falling again, shrouding the area in chilly drizzle. The rain dampened visibility, which was a huge drawback for them. In this rain, a drone couldn't transmit images clearly, and even a patrol vehicle would be at a disadvantage.

But as Dylan drove to the southernmost three access points, spaced a few miles apart, where they were going to search, Grace told herself not to focus on the negatives.

Focus on the outcome. Everyone was waiting for that. The victims and their families deserved it. And in Minnesota, Zach and the director were waiting and hoping to get news of it.

They climbed into the car and sped into the darkness, with Grace automatically checking again and again that she had what she needed. Her phone, a map printout, her gun, her handcuffs. All the equipment to catch a killer.

Jonas Sudbury had not yet been cleared, and had been taken down to the holding cells, but Grace had requested that he should be treated with care. The police who were manning the station had agreed to bring him some dinner and a soda. The officer had been heading out as they had left, on that exact mission.

If Jonas was not the killer, which she was now convinced to be true, then he'd given them invaluable information. But only a physical check would prove if the killer was at work.

There was the first access point, a small signpost, barely visible in the gloom.

"I'll drop you here, and go on to the second?" Dylan asked.

Grace consulted her map.

The first and the second were only a mile apart. The third was about five miles further, and down a longer road.

"I'll check both these," she said. "I can move between them. Your knee is a problem. I don't want you to hurt it worse. Just go to the third. We can stay in touch if we need to re-check."

Looking at the map, Dylan nodded.

"Yeah, I guess that makes the most sense. Okay then. We'll stay in touch."

Grace climbed out, as the headlights swung away. Walking through the damp, clingy ground, hearing the rush of the river ahead, she headed down, checking the path for any sign of footprints, but finding none.

She shone her flashlight ahead, reaching the river itself, seeing the water was dark and murky. There was the small notice advertising swimming access, looking old and tumbledown.

Grace followed the trail along the riverbank, flashlight in hand, scanning for any sign of anyone nearby. The rain was picking up again, and she could feel the cold seeping through her body, even though her jacket kept most of the water out.

The only noise was the sound of the water and the occasional chirping of crickets.

There was nobody here. Time to go to the second meeting point.

She trudged back to the road, and broke into a jog as she traversed the asphalt, her legs quickly covering the distance. She noticed a car parked along the way, but it was on the opposite side of the road. Even so, just in case, she took note of the license plate.

A couple of minutes later, she'd reached the next access point and was heading down the path.

She shone her flashlight around, wishing that someone would radio in with good news, that one of the search party would find this killer. This site, too, seemed empty, although she was going to check every part of it, and would head down to the river along this grassy, steep, and disused trail.

As she began going down, she saw a shadow, coming up.

Someone was trudging up from the river, and Grace tensed immediately, swinging her flashlight in that direction. Who was this person? Were they someone to watch out for?

The man did not look particularly big or strong. His shoulders were hunched, and he looked tired. But Grace knew she needed to make sure.

She shone her flashlight in his direction.

"Stop right there, sir! Please identify yourself?"

The man didn't stop. He staggered toward her, stumbling as he walked, coughing violently.

"I nearly drowned," he husked. "I was tied up, but I got free. I'm injured. I was poisoned. Help me! Please!"

Grace rushed up to him, worry flaring. Were they too late? If the victim had escaped, then so had the killer, and it meant they'd have to start the search anew.

"Can you breathe? Are you able to see okay?" she asked, noticing he was veering sideways as if he was drunk.

It was only then that she smelled the whiff of sour chemical poison emanating from him, a deathly reek.

And saw the maddened light in his eyes as he grabbed her.

CHAPTER THIRTY TWO

The poisonous reek from his clothing, from his skin, was sharp and acrid, and the smell made Grace gasp. His hands were lethally strong and while his left hand was grabbing her right wrist with astonishing strength, his other hand had clamped around her neck.

No time to get her gun. Grace knew this misjudgment could cost her everything.

She'd been too quick to feel sympathy for this man, who seemed so ill. Her soft heart had landed her in a dangerous predicament, and now, she was going to pay for it.

The man's grip was tight, and his strength was unexpected. She kicked and punched, using the evasive maneuvers that she'd practiced a hundred times over in her FBI training sessions, trying to hit any vulnerable spot, but he was like a rock, unyielding to her efforts.

"Cop," he hissed out. "I knew I'd find you, like vermin, creeping around. Trying to stop me. I won't be stopped. I will do what I need to. I have a plan, whatever it takes."

Dammit, if he didn't have her by the throat, she could try to argue with him, use logic, try to talk him down from this place of paranoia and killing intent. But it was all she could do to gasp in a choking breath as his grip adjusted, and then tightened. The flashlight fell from her grasp as he twisted harder. It was another potential weapon, gone, now lying on the muddy grass, as they struggled in its beam.

She kicked out, knowing she needed to get in a hard blow, to hurt him, because a sudden shock of pain was the only thing that might deflect his focus from the need to kill.

But her attempt was futile. His grip on her throat was like steel, cutting off her air supply and making it hard for her to think straight. Her vision was starting to blur, and she knew that if she didn't act fast, she would pass out, and then it would be over.

Don't give up, she told herself. Keep fighting. You owe it to the victims. You owe it to whoever he's going to target next.

And you owe it to whoever he's just buried, she reminded herself, as the blood pounded in her ears. He had been coming from the river, and if she was going to save Nolan Carruthers, she had to stop him now.

When struggling wouldn’t work, she needed to try the opposite.

Words of advice from a particularly brutal and almost forgotten training session surfaced in her mind.

That might work. Instead of struggling against him, Grace took that advice. She dug into the ground with all her strength and she shoved her weight into him, flinging herself toward him, hoping that since he was braced against her, this surprise move would unbalance him.

And it worked. The man stumbled backward, falling onto one knee, his grip on her throat wrenching away so that Grace could gasp in a lungful of air. She coughed and sputtered, her throat burning from the pressure he had applied.

Before he could regain his footing, she kicked him in the stomach with all her might. She didn't think the blow would do more than slow him down, but she was surprised.

He gave a howl of pain and collapsed onto the ground, writhing in agony.

The poisons, Grace realized, as she rushed in, grabbing the handcuffs off her belt, knowing that this gave her the chance she needed, and the only one she would get. The poisons that reeked from his skin must have been in his system, and her well placed kick had crashed into inflamed flesh, and even this maddened man couldn't withstand that pain.

She got one cuff around his wrist, a knee in his back, dragging the other arm behind him with all her strength. But he was regrouping fast. He tugged his arm away from her with an enraged yell. Grace's feet dug into the mud as she battled for purchase to counter his strength. She had to contain the frenzied struggles of this half-insane, and seriously sick man. Whatever it took, she had to take him down. She wrenched his arm sideways, hoping to get another blow to his stomach, but he was too quick, twisting away, countering with a chopping blow that hammered her arm.

Numbness and then pain flooded through her but she hung on, fighting ferociously for the balance and strength she needed to take this last action.

Using everything she had left, Grace scrambled backward, pulling him with her, using the leverage he provided to get her feet under her. She yanked his arm back, avoiding a flailing kick. She could do it; she was just inches away. She had to contain him. The rushing of water was telling her clearly that time was running out for his victim.

And then, as she struggled, arms burning, she heard footsteps behind her. A flashlight beam veered her way and a familiar cry rang out.

“Grace!”

Dylan. He'd checked the other site and come back. His knee looked even worse now. He was barely able to put weight on it as he limped through the mud. But he was coming, as fast as he could.

“Here!” Her voice was raspy, but she managed to shout in reply. Relief filled her as he staggered toward her, grabbing the man's other arm, tugging it so that the cuffs clicked shut.

"Hold him," Grace said, her voice hoarse and breathless. "Keep him there. I've got to go and find Nolan Carruthers!"

"I'll hold him," Dylan shouted, grabbing the cuffs firmly and bracing himself on his good leg as he got onto the radio, calling for backup.

There wasn't time for backup to be any use in saving the victim, though. This, she'd need to do on her own.

She picked up her flashlight from the mud, and ran down to the river, shining it in front of her, trying to follow the footprints the killer had left.

But the mud was too soft, too deep. The prints faded out and then vanished completely as the noise of the river grew louder.

She had lost the trail. But she wasn't going to give up. She ran along the riverbank, scanning the water's edge, hoping to spot some sign of the missing man. She shone her flashlight over the flowing water, scanning for any sign of the victim.

Buried in mud and covered with water. But there must be some sign of him.

Train your eyes, she told herself as she ran through the shallows, looking in every direction, desperate to know where he lay under the cold, flooding wavelets. Train them to see what's there. Look beyond the water.

Master your terrain.

She continued to scan the water's edge, shining her light into the murky depths, hoping to catch a glimpse of something that would lead her to him. And then, just as she was about to give up hope, she saw it. Nothing more than the faintest parting of the shallow water, as if it was flowing over a rock. But the shape reminded her of a buried person.

She rushed over to it, reaching into the cold water, and her hand touched skin, grabbing onto it with all her strength, pulling with all her might. The mud was thick and heavy and it seemed to suck him down and hold him in.

But she battled, pulling at the dead weight of him, tugging him out of the muddy hollow where he'd been left, sick with fear that she was too late.

Then, with a squelch and a splash, she had him. He was free from his grave. Grabbing his tied arms, she hauled him out of the water, fighting the mud, pulling and twisting as she got him to the bank, ripping the soaked gag from his mouth.

And then, he was convulsing, coughing, and choking. Water spurted from his mouth and nose, but he was breathing at least, breathing on his own. He was alive, and he had survived.

The killer's murderous spree was over, and the final victim - at last - had been saved.

CHAPTER THIRTY THREE

The coffee machine at the local hospital was doing a fine job, Grace thought, as she cupped her hands around the steaming mug, her second so far, and there was no guarantee she wouldn't go back for a third.

Nolan Carruthers had been rushed here, and doctors were monitoring him carefully. Grace had been very concerned about the poisons that had leaked into his body and his lungs. But luckily the strength of the flowing river had acted in his favor, and a lot of the toxins seemed to have been washed out of the gag.

He wasn't in danger, and his lungs were clear. The doctors were talking about one more night in the hospital to monitor him, and then it looked like he'd be discharged.

With his wife and young daughter now in the ward, visiting him, Grace felt a warmth in her heart that one family at least was still whole.

As for the killer, he was in the ICU and they were not sure if he was going to survive. While handcuffed, shortly after the police van had arrived, he had collapsed. It seemed, from what the doctor had muttered to the policeman on guard outside the ward, that he'd been consuming the poison himself. The toxic load in his body had abruptly tipped over, perhaps due to the sudden stress of capture. Now, with multiple organ failure, the prognosis was poor.

If he lived, it would be as a permanent invalid.

His name was Chas Williams, and he'd lost his son a year ago. Grace had pieced together from what the nurses remembered that the son had been swimming long distances in the most polluted parts of the river, despite warnings and cautions. He'd passed out one day while in the water. He'd been rescued, but the water in his lungs had caused pneumonia and he'd died as a result.

It was a sad story, but sadder still that his father's psychotic break had caused so many other deaths. Police were already searching Chas's home, and had uncovered a stash of poisons, as well as cotton wool, gags, and ropes.

And the surprise hero of the hour, whose research would help local police enormously in their case against Lewes Inc., was Jonas Sudbury, the journalist whose blog had blown the whistle.

Grace knew that he would be hailed as a local celebrity, and that this turnaround would allow him to get back on his feet and reclaim his life, after having so much ripped away by the corruption and cover-ups that had derailed his career.

An uneven thumping noise got her turning her head. Dylan was walking through to the waiting room, with the aid of a crutch, after having his knee strapped up.

"How's it feeling?" she asked in concern. She hoped that no permanent damage was done.

"Doc says it's good. I must rest it for a week or two, keep wearing this brace for a while, and then he says it should be fine from there on. No bad damage done. I'll just have to unpack my stuff more slowly than I was planning to."

Grace gave a sympathetic smile. "I hope that isn't too stressful. I wish I was closer to you, because if I was, I'd come over and help out. But please, don't be sad about this, at least, not more than you can help. Any time you need to talk, or you're feeling down, just call me. I mean it. Please."

He nodded in thanks. "I appreciate that. And, who knows? When things have settled and I've gotten a new start, perhaps I should move to Minnesota. There's nothing keeping me down here now," he acknowledged wryly. "I see my dad once every couple of months, but that's a four-hour car ride to another state. Might as well be an airplane ride."

"Nothing keeping you down here except the winters," she joked. "I'm not looking forward to going back up to that brutal cold in Minnesota. Maybe I should move down here."

Dylan looked concerned. "You? Move here? I thought -" His voice trailed off and he looked uncomfortable.

"That I was living with someone? Yes. I thought so too." With a sigh, Grace acknowledged her own situation. "But now, I'm not sure. And I'd rather spend some time alone, and figure out what I really want, than be stuck in a relationship that's going nowhere," she admitted.

Dylan frowned. "Well, I'm just a phone call away for you. It sounds as if you have some tough decisions to make when you get back home."

"Tough, yes. But I think I'll make the right decision." Grace nodded slowly and she knew, deep inside, that her mind was made up. "We need some time apart. It's not working, and it's never going to be easy to call it off. But sometimes, it has to be done."

"True," Dylan said somberly.

Grace checked the time. Her late night flight back home was booked, and she needed to get to the airport. Tomorrow, she'd have a tough day when she told Tyler that she was moving out, and she wanted a break from their relationship.

"See you soon, I guess," she said, pressing the button on her phone to call the Uber that she knew would take only a minute to arrive, in this downtown setting.

"See you soon."

They stared at each other and for a moment, Grace felt awkward. She wanted to give Dylan a hug. But perhaps they weren't yet on that footing. Perhaps just a goodbye would be more suitable. But still, they'd been through so much. And a handshake seemed way too formal.

While she was fretting over the best way to handle this moment, Dylan took a limping step toward her, held out his arms, and they exchanged a brief hug.

It felt good to have him hold her tight for a moment. It felt like they were a team. And Grace was looking forward to seeing him again, even though she knew it would only be when there was another serious crime somewhere in the Mississippi River region.

As she walked away, heading for the Uber, she decided that being here, in Arkansas, had clearly shown her something.

Her mother's death had been traumatic to her, and it was a reason why she'd always avoided this state and never made any plans to travel here. She'd never wanted to. She'd always had an ugly picture of it in her mind.

But, being down here had made her revise her views on the area, which she'd always thought of as high in random crime.

It wasn't. The serial case she'd just handled was the exception, and it had shown her all over again what a peaceful place this area generally was. Had her mother's murder really been a random crime? It hadn't been a serial crime, like this one. In that case, what had it been for? Was there something she was missing?

Grace promised herself that when she got back home, she was going to take another look at her mother's cold case, and see if anything had been overlooked.

After all, if she found the courage to move out of their apartment and take a break from the relationship with Tyler, she'd have some spare time on her hands.

Now, she knew how she could use it.

NOW AVAILABLE!

NEARLY FREE
(A Grace Ford FBI Thriller—Book Three)

With a string of unsolved murders up and down the Mississippi River, the FBI assembles a task force, assigning their best Minnesota field agent, Grace Ford, to partner with an agent from their Louisiana office. Despite their culture clash, the two must work together to traverse the country, crack the hardest cases—and to stop the next killer before it's too late.

Another body is found floating on a barge downriver, and Grace realizes right away it's the mark of a new killer, stalking the Mississippi—and that she must navigate interstate authority conflicts if she has any chance of saving the next victim in time.

"Molly Black has written a taut thriller that will keep you on the edge of your seat… I absolutely loved this book and can't wait to read the next book in the series!"
—Reader review for Girl One: Murder

NEARLY FREE is book #3 in a long anticipated new series by critically-acclaimed and #1 bestselling mystery and suspense author Molly Black, whose books have received over 2,000 five-star reviews and ratings.

A page-turning and harrowing crime thriller featuring a brilliant and tortured FBI agent, the Grace Ford series is a riveting mystery, packed with non-stop action, suspense, twists and turns, revelations, and driven by a breakneck pace that will keep you flipping pages late into the night. Fans of Rachel Caine, Teresa Driscoll and Robert Dugoni are sure to fall in love.

Future Books in the series are also available.

“I binge read this book. It hooked me in and didn't stop till the last few pages… I look forward to reading more!”
—Reader review for Found You

“I loved this book! Fast-paced plot, great characters and interesting insights into investigating cold cases. I can't wait to read the next book!”
—Reader review for Girl One: Murder

“Very good book… You will feel like you are right there looking for the kidnapper! I know I will be reading more in this series!”
—Reader review for Girl One: Murder

“This is a very well written book and holds your interest from page 1… Definitely looking forward to reading the next one in the series, and hopefully others as well!”
—Reader review for Girl One: Murder

“Wow, I cannot wait for the next in this series. Starts with a bang and just keeps going.”
—Reader review for Girl One: Murder

“Well written book with a great plot, one that will keep you up at night. A page turner!”
—Reader review for Girl One: Murder

“A great suspense that keeps you reading… can't wait for the next in this series!”
—Reader review for Found You

“Sooo soo good! There are a few unforeseen twists… I binge read this like I binge watch Netflix. It just sucks you in.”
—Reader review for Found You

Molly Black

Bestselling author Molly Black is author of the MAYA GRAY FBI suspense thriller series, comprising nine books (and counting); of the RYLIE WOLF FBI suspense thriller series, comprising six books; of the TAYLOR SAGE FBI suspense thriller series, comprising eight books; of the KATIE WINTER FBI suspense thriller series, comprising eleven books (and counting); of the RUBY HUNTER FBI suspense thriller series, comprising five books (and counting); of the CAITLIN DARE FBI suspense thriller series, comprising five books (and counting); of the REESE LINK mystery series, comprising five books (and counting); of the CLAIRE KING FBI suspense thriller series, comprising five books (and counting); and of the GRACE FORD FBI suspense thriller series, comprising five books (and counting).

An avid reader and lifelong fan of the mystery and thriller genres, Molly loves to hear from you, so please feel free to visit www.mollyblackauthor.com to learn more and stay in touch.

BOOKS BY MOLLY BLACK

GRACE FORD MYSTERY SERIES
NEARLY MINE (Book #1)
NEARLY SAFE (Book #2)
NEARLY FREE (Book #3)
NEARLY GONE (Book #4)
NEARLY HIS (Book #5)

CLAIRE KING MYSTERY SERIES
ONCE HE SEES (Book #1)
ONCE HE LONGS (Book #2)
ONCE HE TAKES (Book #3)
ONCE HE FEELS (Book #4)
ONCE HE KNOWS (Book #5)

MAYA GRAY MYSTERY SERIES
GIRL ONE: MURDER (Book #1)
GIRL TWO: TAKEN (Book #2)
GIRL THREE: TRAPPED (Book #3)
GIRL FOUR: LURED (Book #4)
GIRL FIVE: BOUND (Book #5)
GIRL SIX: FORSAKEN (Book #6)
GIRL SEVEN: CRAVED (Book #7)
GIRL EIGHT: HUNTED (Book #8)
GIRL NINE: GONE (Book #9)

RYLIE WOLF FBI SUSPENSE THRILLER
FOUND YOU (Book #1)
CAUGHT YOU (Book #2)
SEE YOU (Book #3)
WANT YOU (Book #4)
TAKE YOU (Book #5)
DARE YOU (Book #6)

TAYLOR SAGE FBI SUSPENSE THRILLER

DON'T LOOK (Book #1)
DON'T BREATHE (Book #2)
DON'T RUN (Book #3)
DON'T FLINCH (Book #4)
DON'T REMEMBER (Book #5)
DON'T TELL (Book #6)

KATIE WINTER FBI SUSPENSE THRILLER
SAVE ME (Book #1)
REACH ME (Book #2)
HIDE ME (Book #3)
BELIEVE ME (Book #4)
HELP ME (Book #5)
FORGET ME (Book #6)
HOLD ME (Book #7)
PROTECT ME (Book #8)
REMEMBER ME (Book #9)
CATCH ME (Book #10)
WATCH ME (Book #11)

RUBY HUNTER FBI SUSPENSE THRILLER
IF I RUN (Book #1)
IF I TELL (Book #2)
IF I LIVE (Book #3)
IF I FORGET (Book #4)
IF I RETURN (Book #5)

CAITLIN DARE FBI SUSPENSE THRILLER
COME GET ME (Book #1)
COME FIND ME (Book #2)
COME TAKE ME (Book #3)
COME CATCH ME (Book #4)
COME SAVE ME (Book #5)

REESE LINK MYSTERY
BEYOND REASON (Book #1)
BEYOND REACH (Book #2)
BEYOND REPAIR (Book #3)
BEYOND DOUBT (Book #4)
BEYOND NORMAL (Book #5)

Made in the USA
Coppell, TX
08 March 2024

29885319R00085